Eliza is forced into marriage with no idea her life will change for the better. Married less than a year, her unwilling rake of a husband is surprisingly kind to her—until his sudden death. The widowed Countess of Sunderland remains under her in-laws' protection to raise her newborn daughter. But her abusive father is on the brink of financial ruin and has plans for another wedding.

Nathaniel, Viscount of Pendleton, gains his title at the age of twelve. His kindly but shrewd estate manager becomes father and mentor, instilling in the boy an astute sense of responsibility and compassion for his tenants. Fifteen years later, his family urges him to visit London and seek a wife. The ideal doesn't appeal to him, but his sense of duty tells him it is the next logical step.

Lord Pendleton stumbles upon Eliza on the road, defending an elderly woman against ruffians. After rescuing the exquisite damsel in distress, he finds himself smitten. But Nate soon realizes he must discover the dark secrets of her past to truly save the woman he loves.

Other Books by Aubrey Wynne

The Earl of Sunderland
(Once Upon A Widow, Book 1)

A Wicked Earl's Widow
(Once Upon A Widow, Book 2)

Rhapsody and Rebellion
(Once Upon A Widow, Book 3)

Earl of Darby

(Once Upon A Widow, Book 4)

Rolf's Quest
(A Medieval Encounter #1)

Dante's Gift
(A Chicago Christmas novella, Book 1)

Saving Grace
(A Small Town Romance #1)

For the Love of Laura Beth
(Small Town Romance #2
A Chicago Christmas, Book 4)

A Wicked Earl's Widow

By
Aubrey Wynne

ISBN-13: 978-1-946560-16-2

ISBN-10: 1-946560-16-2

Editing by The Editing Hall

Cover Art by Taylor Sullivan, Imagination Uncovered

Formatting by Anessa Books

Acknowledgments

Once again, a huge thank you to my most dedicated readers: Renate Pennington, Debbie Kolins, Sharon Martin, Deb Jones Diem, Rebecca Cobb Jones, Pauline Frost, and Nancy Pennick. To my assistant, Nicole Ulery, who has been my right-hand woman and partner in crazy, my deepest thanks.

To my mom and sister, who support me and fix all my goofy plot ideas and read everything. I couldn't publish a book without them. And my husband, who patiently goes without a wife for weeks at a time when she crawls into the writing cave.

"Death is the veil which those who love call life;
They sleep and it is lifted."

Percy Bysshe Shelley

Chapter One

Mid April 1818
Falsbury Estate
Lincolnshire, England

Eliza rubbed the polished marble set in the stone wall, one gloved hand tracing her husband's name. A tear rolled down her cheek as Althea clutched at her skirts, the toddler pulling and fidgeting in the quiet mausoleum.

Here lies the body of
Carson Roker, Earl of Sunderland
Son of Allan Roker, Marquess of Falsbury
16 June 1815
Aged 31 years

The Lord hath given him rest from all his enemies.
11 Samuel 7:1

"Oh, how I miss your laughter and strength. I envy the fact your demon no longer chases you, but mine is close on our heels." The chill of the surrounding limestone seeped into her bones. "How shall I keep him at bay?" She sniffled and bent down to touch her daughter's plump cheeks. The tiny face turned up, two matching dimples peeking out from the corners of her mouth as she smiled. "Can you see how beautiful your little girl grows each day, Carson? Your mother says she has your coloring and my eyes, your boundless energy and my common sense. A perfect combination, yes?"

Althea tugged impatiently at her skirts again. "Mama, go now." One chubby finger pointed toward the small garden behind the mausoleum. The stained glass at the end of the building shed a pastel rainbow over the budding flowers and short rock wall.

"Yes, my sweet, you may play."

The girl ran toward the back exit then stopped. Her small feet hopped on the reflecting kaleidoscope of colors, the sun's rays gleaming through the painted glass.

"Yewow," she said and hopped again to another color. "Gween." Another hop. "Bwue."

"Very good. Only two, and you know all your colors." She brushed back the glossy midnight curls that rebelled against the confinements of hat and ribbons. The lacy plum bonnet matched the girl's sparkling eyes.

"I pick fowers."

"Yes, go pick some flowers. Not too many and only those that have bloomed."

Eliza sat heavily on the bench across from Carson's epitaph. Althea squealed in delight at the yellow blossoms clinging to the locked gate. One of these days, the enclosure would not be tall enough to hold her precocious daughter.

The monthly visits were a comforting ritual. At first, she'd come to be alone and grieve. To mourn the death of her husband taken after a year of marriage, leaving behind a pregnant widow. To mourn the affection she'd dreamed of all her young life, only to have it snatched away so quickly. To mourn the father who would never hold his child, and the child who would never know the man her father had become.

Theirs had been an arranged marriage. A duty for Carson, the Earl of Sunderland, a twin who had tried to pass his responsibilities on to his brother. An escape for Lady Eliza, daughter of the Marquess of Landonshire, from a brutal father and a lonely childhood. Her father had not cared about the roguish character of his future son-in-law. His priority was increasing his wealth and improving the family connection.

Carson's reputation as a rake had not been exaggerated. Yet Eliza had sensed a generous but vulnerable heart in her husband, cleverly disguised by sarcasm and alcohol. The wedding night had been brief and perfunctory. The groom had been gentle but distant. She had seen little of her husband during the days following until...

She smiled, remembering the first gift he'd given her. A bouquet of flowers he'd picked at dawn as he stumbled home after one month of marriage. He had knocked at her door, one hand behind his back, smelling of alcohol and the clubs. After mumbling an apology for missing the previous night's obligations, he'd handed her a bouquet of crushed violets.

"They matched your eyes."

She had gazed from the mangled petals to the contrite man intensely interested in his dusty boots. As she put the flowers to her nose, the sweet scent was her undoing. The tears had come unbidden and swift as Eliza clutched the first gift she'd ever received from a man. It had also been the earl's undoing, he had told her, when she gave him a brilliant watery smile.

"By Christ, woman, if you weep over wilted flowers, you'll flood the Thames when I give you jewels."

She'd only nodded her head and sniffled. Carson had pulled out a handkerchief and awkwardly dried her cheeks. As she looked up at him, their eyes met and held. Something passed between them at that moment. Two lost souls finding the same purchase in a storm they'd battled all their lives. He'd kissed her then. His lips gentle and sweet. It had been a different kind of kiss from her wedding night. Not polite and careful but questioning and heavy with need. Her first taste of passion.

After that he'd brought her a small token each time he returned. After six months, his visits to the clubs had become less frequent. He would appear at breakfast with steady hands and clear eyes. Carson's father had given Eliza the credit for his transformation. She'd only shook her head. They would never understand the empty space she and Carson filled for one another. He gave her security, protection from a life of abuse, and laughter. He taught her about desire and that all men were not callous and cruel. She leaned on him, pushed him to be better through her adoration, her constant understanding.

"For the first time in my life, I feel like someone's hero. You make me want to be the man I see in your eyes."

They had forged a kinship and found a tentative, fragile love. Eliza had been so happy, so deliriously happy. Then fate had grasped that happiness by the throat and tried to strangle it. But Eliza ignored the devious hand dealt her and instead rejoiced in Carson's child.

Over the past months, this cold place had become a warm refuge. In the beginning, she told him of his family and reported the latest on-dits. He'd always loved the gossip. It was a way to say thank you to the first man who'd shown her kindness and affection. A way to battle the loneliness after the riding accident and his abrupt death. As time passed, she shared her thoughts almost like a verbal diary. He was close to her in this vault. Words that would never pass her lips elsewhere, echoed against these walls. Here Eliza could clear her mind, soothe her soul, and renew her strength. She could feel Carson here, feel him listening and grinning, nodding and frowning.

She had grown content with her life. Her in-laws doted on Althea and held them both with great affection. Lady Falsbury had made it clear her daughter-in-law would always have a home with them. That previous life, full of pain and fear, had begun fading into distant memories.

Yet the past has a way of haunting the present.

"Father sent another letter." Eliza heard the tremble in her own voice and bit her lip. "I know your family is powerful and he cannot hurt me but... He frightens me, Carson."

"Mama," shouted Althea. "Come see my pwetty flowers."

"Coming, Thea." Eliza waved at her daughter and looked back at the stone as if it would continue the conversation.

"You know the end of the war wreaked havoc on Papa's investments. His partner, Mr. Bellum, wants an heir and respectability in his dotage, a young wife with connections. The old man has increased his bid to marry me." Eliza gripped the bench, her nails scraping against the ironwork, turning her knuckles white. "I've stood firm, Carson. Even when he threatened to beat Mama every night, I stood firm for our daughter."

Althea screeched and called again, her voice shrill now. "Mama, Mama!"

Fear wrapped around Eliza's heart and squeezed. She picked up her skirt and ran to the small garden. A man sat on the stone fence, his back to her with a tall black hat covering his head. Althea writhed on his lap. Her violet eyes darkened with rage as she fought against the stranger who held her. Eliza could feel the evil seeping from the figure and knew those icy gray eyes before he turned to face her. His steely cold gaze spurred her into action.

"Althea," she called as she pulled on the little girl's arms. "Give her back, you monster."

"Let's not frighten the poor chit. I am her grandfather." Lord Landonshire stood, Althea trapped in his firm grip. "Why don't you introduce us?"

"What are you doing here? What do you want?" Her heart raced and she struggled for calm.

He'd aged, the lines deep and craggy around his eyes and mouth. Life had not gone his way the past few years. And when things did not go well for the Marquess of Landonshire, someone always paid a price. A tremor ran through her body, her fingers curled, wanting to scratch the brute's eyes out. She would not cower, would not feed his appetite for fear. At this moment, Eliza could kill him without a second thought to save her baby.

"Oh, come now. You know what I want. How many letters have I sent?" He tossed the girl up in the air, her skirt billowing out as she descended back into her grandfather's arms. With a grunt, Althea gave a mighty kick and caught her captive in the chin.

Cold terror clawed at Eliza's stomach. She watched him grip Althea around the waist with one arm and stroke her neck with the back of his free hand.

"Let her go. Please let her go."

"Hmm... I believe my granddaughter is due for a visit. It's past time, and I know your mother would love to see how she's grown. Those small portraits you've sent don't do the girl justice." He smiled, his yellow teeth glistening in the afternoon sunshine. "I can still bring you to heel, you damned little trollop."

She set her shoulders straight, her chin out. "Kidnapping is beyond even you, I would think."

"I'm a marquess and her grandfather, you lackwit. No one would accuse me of kidnapping. But it would certainly get you back under my roof." His smile held no warmth. "And we both know I would be able to convince you once you were home."

"You've already sold the property from my dowry. How much more could you possible need?"

"It's gone. In a moment of desperation, I hoped to double that amount. It would have been just enough if I had won that last hand. I still say the scoundrel cheated." He shrugged. "So here we are. As my daughter, you must obey me. At least until you are twenty-one."

"I will not marry that vile, ancient man and bring my daughter into a home without love. She is happy and well-cared for and—"

"I don't give a bloody hell where the brat goes. It's you I need. I'm at a standstill and in need of blunt. This marriage will set things right for me." His fingers slowly wrapped around Althea's neck and stroked the taut muscles as the girl swallowed. "Such a fragile thing, isn't she? How easily I was able to take her."

A sob escaped Eliza's throat. She reached out, grabbed Althea's arms, and pulled with all her might. Landonshire let go of the pair and they flew backward, landing hard on the grass. Althea clutched at Eliza's neck, whimpering and hiding her face.

"Watch over your daughter closely when you put her to bed and pull the mauve counterpane over her tiny body. Beware if she wanders while you read under your favorite oak. It overlooks that lovely swan fountain, yes?" He stood over them, blocking the sun, his face shadowed with only the pale flash of his eyes and teeth visible. "Accidents happen so quickly."

"My dower share, I receive it quarterly. It's yours." She hated the whine in her voice, the fear that gave her father his strength. Panic overtook her courage as more horrid thoughts crowded her brain. How did he know what Althea's bedroom looked like? Had he been watching them during their afternoons in the garden? "M-my solicitor will take care of the transfer. Just leave us alone." Her voice fell to a whisper. "*Please.*"

"Negotiations are no longer an option. You know what you must do." He bent down and placed his hands on her shoulders, raising her to a sitting position. She clutched Althea to her chest as he pulled her to her feet.

"I understand the entire family will be in London next week. What luck! It happens I will be visiting my partner. I will call on you at Lord Falsbury's townhouse and suggest a ride to give you all the news from home. We will spend a pleasant afternoon with Mr. Bellum and announce the betrothal that evening. Do you understand?"

Eliza tried to stem the quaver that had begun in her legs. Be strong. The marquess will not let him hurt Althea.

His fingers gripped her jaw and squeezed, his short nails digging into her soft skin. She shut her eyes against the familiar pain, holding back the tears of anger and frustration.

"Do. You. Understand?" he hissed.

She nodded, knowing there would be bruises.

"That's my sweet girl." He kissed the top of her head and gave her a wink. "It will be good to see you again, Eliza. Perhaps after you're wed, I'll let your mother come stay with you for an extended visit. If you both behave. It will be my wedding gift to you and Mr. Bellum." He stooped to pick up his hat, brushed it off, and strode off whistling.

"Not to go back is somewhat to advance, and men must walk, at least, before they dance."

Alexander Pope

Chapter Two

Eliza stared at the red marks along her jaw, and the nightmare came flooding back. The bruises, broken bones, and constant confinement. She closed her eyes, trying to push the memories to the dark corners of her mind. Mama's gaunt face haunted her dreams these days. Guilt, she supposed, for being the one to escape. She prayed God would not let her mother suffer for Eliza's lack of obedience. But since this afternoon, she'd wondered if she'd ever had a choice.

She dressed slowly for dinner, choosing a somber gray dress to fit her mood. If the marquess and marchioness would allow Althea to remain with them, she would obey her father. Her throat swelled and she swallowed the lump, realizing her relationship with Althea would become distant. Another woman would raise her precious child. But the idea of her daughter growing up under Landonshire's thumb horrified her. She gritted her teeth, hardening her resolve that Althea would have a better childhood than her mother. That vile man would always be in Eliza's life, watching over her until the day he died. She would never escape his controlling reach, and she could not live looking over her shoulder, wondering where he might appear next. If only Carson had not fallen from that horse...

What-ifs did not keep her daughter safe. She straightened her shoulders, clutched the powder and brush, and attempted to cover the red marks. Lady Falsbury was sharp-eyed and meticulous, noticing every small detail that concerned her house and family. The older woman would not let her go without a fight if she thought Eliza had been coerced in any way. The decision was difficult enough without her in-laws trying to come to her rescue. She would survive. Perhaps the decrepit Mr. Bellum was in ill health. Mayhap he was even kind. Her father might even keep his word and allow her mother respite with Eliza. She blinked back the tears and concentrated on covering the dull red prints marring her pale skin. It seemed her fairy tale had ended without a happily ever after.

―――⌒⌒―――

"My dear, you look pale. Would you like a cordial?" Lady Falsbury's eyes narrowed. "Are you feeling well?"

"Yes, thank you. I'm a bit tired. Althea's well of energy is bottomless, but she's finally spent." She sat down in a chair on the opposite side of the room, presenting her profile with the faintest mark. And prayed her face was shadowed. "I have already kissed her goodnight and sent her to bed."

"I brought back a gift for my granddaughter. Since I haven't seen her in two weeks, I told the governess to bring her down for a short while." Lord Falsbury gave her a sheepish grin. "I hope you don't mind."

"Really Chester, if you were concerned you would have asked her first," chided his wife.

"Strange, that voice sounds more like you, Lydia, than Eliza." He bent with a wicked grin and kissed his wife soundly on the mouth. "That should stop any arguments for a bit. You'll get your trinket later." He wiggled his bushy silver eyebrows.

Lady Falsbury blushed and pushed him away, the opal in her ring sparkling green and blue in the firelight. "Sir, you are still a scoundrel."

"And you still can't resist me." He grinned, his brown eyes twinkling. "Now take a look at my prize purchase."

The older couple was an inspiration to Eliza. Proof love could survive over time. They cared for one another, were thoughtful toward each other, and still affectionate. She and Carson might have achieved that special kind of bond, given time. The shared looks that never needed a word spoken, the clasped hands as they ascended the stairs each night, private jokes, and secret smiles.

Falsbury bent behind the settee and pulled out a box. He lifted the lid and took out a doll, half the size of Althea, and set it on a side table near the hearth. Springy black curls framed a porcelain face with painted violet eyes. Dressed in a deep purple muslin gown with pale rose ribbons threading the bodice, the doll closely resembled its new owner. Any other time, Eliza would have enjoyed watching her daughter receive such a gift. She prayed the toy was enough distraction to keep Althea from mentioning this afternoon's disaster. Please, Lord. Let me protect her.

A gasp pulled her attention from the doll. Althea stood in the doorway, her hands covering her mouth, toes peeking out from beneath her night-rail. Like lightning, she streaked across the room, babbling as she focused on the doll.

"Is me! Is me!" She hugged her miniature, jumping up and down. "Gwandpappa, fo' me?"

"Well, I did consider keeping it for myself, but I don't think she'd be nearly as content." He squatted down and held out his arms. "Come and show Papa Falsy how much you like her."

Althea carefully set the doll down, adjusted the tiny straw bonnet with pink satin ribbons, and then threw herself into Lord Falsbury's arms. "Now that's the kind of gratitude every female in this household should exhibit."

Lady Falsbury rolled her eyes but chuckled. "When we go to London, we will visit my modiste and order some matching outfits. In the meantime, she must have a name."

Althea nodded, a serious expression on her sleepy face. She rubbed her eyes, yawned, and picked the doll up again. "A pwetty name. I sweep wif her?" She rubbed her eyes with a chubby fist.

Eliza nodded. "Now give us a hug and kiss good night. It's past your bedtime."

The little girl squeezed her grandfather's neck once more and gave him a sloppy kiss, making a loud noise against his cheek and giggling. In return, he tickled her belly and sent her off to her grandmother. "G'night, gwandmama. Wuv you sooo much."

"And I love you sooo much more." She wrapped the little one in a tight hug. "We'll see you in the morning."

Althea walked to her mother and leaned on her tiptoes to give her a kiss. Her foot caught on the chair leg, tipping her forward and pushing her forehead against her Eliza's downturned face. She grimaced at the impact on her sore jaw but quickly recovered, casting a side-glance at her mother-in-law. In a light voice, she said, "Sweet dreams, my darling. Now go with Miss Watkins."

The governess smiled, dimples poking her round cheeks. She tucked a stray lock of fading auburn hair back into her bun and squatted down. Her light blue eyes were warm as she held out her arms to Althea. "Come along, my little one. I have the perfect story to send you off to Slumber Land."

When the door was shut, Falsbury refilled his glass of brandy and sat next to his wife. "Slumber Land, is it?"

"Althea had a nightmare last month and didn't want to close her eyes the next night. Miss Watkins told her to go to Slumber Land when she slept. There were no nightmares allowed there. And passage to this dreamless land is a bedtime story." Eliza smiled. "Lauren is a godsend. She is so good to Althea, and they adore each other. I was lucky to find her."

"She's worth every penny and came highly recommended," agreed the marquess. "Now, shall I escort my two best ladies to dinner?"

His wife held up a hand. "Not until Eliza tells us what happened today."

Two sets of eyes fell on her, one suspicious, one inquiring. Her face burned with shame. "I-I..." What could she say? Her father wanted to marry her off to an elderly rich merchant, and she was happy to accept his proposal? Her heart sank as her plan crumbled along with her bravado. She could not lie to these people who had shown her only kindness. They were her family as much as any blood relative. Besides, Lydia would never believe that Eliza could willingly leave her daughter behind. Tears sprang to her eyes, and she dashed them away with irritation. "Do you promise to listen until I'm finished and not to try to dissuade me?"

"I will stay silent until you have finished but I shall not make any such promises." Lady Falsbury rose and crossed the room, the swish of her umber silk the only noise in the drawing room. She sat next to Eliza, adjusting her lace shawl over her shoulders and smoothing the Vandyke edging, then focused her full attention on her daughter-in-law. "Now, how did you get those marks on your face?"

"I'm not sure where to start." Eliza took a deep breath and let the words tumble out. She began with the letters her father had sent over the last six months and the threats against her mother.

Falsbury interrupted. "By Christ, he's gone through the money from the dowry property?"

How did he know about that? "He... I—"

"Come my dear, do you think the solicitor hired by *my son* would not keep me informed?" The marquess snorted. "Did you know he tried to get Carson to invest in one of his shipping schemes shortly after your wedding?"

Eliza could only shake her head.

"We both believed it was the reason he wanted the match to begin with. When Carson declined the offer, Landonshire got his back up and said there'd be the devil to pay for crossing him." His face softened, and he stopped pacing to stand in front of her. "I apologize. You asked us not to interrupt. Please continue."

Her head pounded. She hadn't known her father had tried to get money so early in the marriage. With an effort she finished her story, ending with the events at the cemetery. By the time she finished, her shoulders ached from the tension but her eyes were again dry. "When I saw his hand on Althea's throat, I-I—"

"Blast and bugger his eyes, he harmed my granddaughter?" Lord Falsbury's pacing had increased as her story progressed. "I'll see him in Dunn territory before the year is up."

"He's already ruined. Nothing you can do will make his situation worse. I feel it's best if I marry Mr. Bellum. If I cooperate, he may allow Mama to come live with me." She held up a hand as her mother-in-law opened her mouth to argue. "I will survive but I cannot allow Althea to grow up in such an environment. I would like to leave her here."

She grasped the older woman's hand. "Please, keep her with you, raise her for me. I will visit as often as possible, but my heart will rest easy knowing she is in your care."

"My dear, under any other circumstance I would agree. But I cannot raise your daughter."

Eliza fought for breath. Would they truly deny her? There was no other way.

"When Carson married you, I finally received the daughter I had prayed for. When I lost my son, you were there for me, comforting and patient." The marchioness took her hand in a firm grip. "I love you as my own and will not see harm come to you. We will not give in to his cork-brained demands."

"I agree with my wife. He's no better than a bully ruffian, and he's made his last threat against my family. He'll float in the Thames before he gets another penny."

"Chester, don't frighten the girl. No one will end up in the river. He's a bitter old man who's lost too many sons," Lady Falsbury said reprovingly. "Leave the bluster for later and come up with a solution."

Eliza laced her shaking fingers together and closed her eyes. This is what she had feared. Yet surprisingly, her racing heart had slowed. She was no longer standing alone against her enemy. They were older and wiser, and she would listen to what they had to say.

The marquess took up his pacing again. "He's got a spy in my household. I'll have my steward look over the books for any new hires, especially those who may have access to our private quarters. And you, my dear, must take a French leave."

Eliza drew in a breath. "Pack up and depart unannounced? But my father is expecting to call on us in London next week. He'll be furious to find an empty house."

Falsbury gave a tight smile. "You misunderstand, my dear. I have every intention of receiving Lord Landonshire next week. He needs to be informed that his daughter and granddaughter have sailed for the colonies. Boston, perhaps."

"Boston? I should run away to America?"

He sighed and shook his head. "That will be our story. At dawn, you will depart for Sunderland Castle. My son is more than capable of keeping the both of you safe, and I am sure his wife will be overjoyed to have her cousin for an extended visit."

Christopher, or Kit as his family called him, had inherited Carson's title on his twin's death. He was married to Eliza's cousin and best friend, Grace. "I do not want to put anyone in danger—"

"There is not a man in England I would put more trust in, even if he were not my son. He faced Napoleon at Waterloo, an aging marquess won't be so difficult." Falsbury grinned as he always did when speaking of Kit's accomplishments. "As soon as you are safely away, we'll find out who is supplying Landonshire with information."

Lydia chimed in. "Tomorrow morning the rest of the household will be informed you have fallen ill. A bit of a spring chill, nothing serious, and Althea will remain in her nursery until we are sure she has not caught it." She put her a finger to her mouth, a habit that told Eliza she was plotting something. "Lauren will need to be told since she'll accompany you, but we won't tell her the destination."

"I'll arrange for a coach without our crest." Falsbury resumed his pacing again, his tall figure emanating power and comfort to both women. "He'll know of someone who can be trusted. With only three outsiders in our confidence, our secret should be safe enough."

"Come my dear, let us have a quiet dinner while we finish the details. I will have a final meal with my daughter." Lydia squeezed her hands, spreading warmth into Eliza's icy fingers. "Whether you like it or not, you are part of our family and will always be treated as such."

"And protected," added Falsbury.

She was done to a cow's thumb, exhaustion and relief creeping through her bones like thick molasses. Peace was all she wanted. All she had ever hoped for in this life. But Eliza had learned the carriage of life had a tendency to take sharp turns, and one had to be ready to grab the leather strap and hold on.

"Seldom, very seldom, does complete truth belong to any human disclosure; seldom can it happen that something is not a little disguised, or a little mistaken."

Jane Austen, *Emma*

Chapter Three

April 1818
Durham, England

The Viscount Pendleton took a deep pull of his ale and raised his tankard high. He threw back his head and added his voice to the drunken patrons of the Bear and Bull Inn.

But the standing toast
That pleased the most
Was the wind that blows
The ship that goes,
And the lass that loves a sailor.

He slammed the metal cup on the wooden table and leaned back in his chair, grinning at his estate steward. "Maxwell, this is one of your better ideas today. Good food, pretty maids"—he slapped a buxom redhead on the bottom as she walked by balancing four mugs—"and fine ale." The girl smiled, winked at him, and moved on to the next table.

"We've earned it, my lord. Work hard, play hard my father always said." Ezra Maxwell raised his own tankard. "To a job well done, sir."

The sound of clanking metal and liquid slopping onto a tabletop joined another round of the maritime song.

"You know I always wanted to be a sailor," Nathaniel said, his voice slurring just a tiny bit. He was sure his steward hadn't noticed.

"Ye can't swim." He leaned forward, eyes squinting as he focused on Nathaniel. "Not to be impertinent but what kind of blasted sailor doesn't swim?"

"The kind who is very careful never to fall off the ship!"

Both men guffawed and slammed their cups together again as plates of mutton and gravy with fresh crusty bread was set before them. Nate took a bite of the tender meat and closed his eyes, the gravy sliding down his throat to answer his growling stomach. The food was surprisingly good and would help sober him up. How did Maxwell manage to find places like this? It wasn't often either of the men overindulged, but this was a celebration.

His investment in the Durham carpet factory had paid off in aces. Pendle Place and the accompanying properties, run to the ground by his father, once again turned a profit. It had taken thirteen years, but Pendleton was a respected family name again.

"I would like to make a toast to the best man in England. Clever, industrious, and loyal. May I never have to make a decision without you." He held up his ale but this time his voice was soft and serious. "You have been like a second father to me. I don't know where I or my mother and sister would be without you this past decade."

"It's not my doing, my lord. You were an astute student and eager to learn." Red seeped up Maxwell's neck and he waved off the compliment. "I only did as my position dictated and fulfilled my duties as estate manager."

"Your *duties* did not include raising a twelve-year-old boy and teaching him what his father never bothered to learn. Mother says if he hadn't died, we'd have lost everything."

Died was a misleading word. The previous viscount had been in a duel after being caught with another man's wife. His father had never been much of a shot, and he succumbed to a chest wound several days later. It had been a long and unpleasant death.

"Your father should never have inherited the title. He was the third son and not suited to such a position of responsibility. He had no head for business." Maxwell stroked his beard with his thumb and two fingers. "Or marriage for that matter. A wanderer's soul, your father had. But he did care for his family, regardless of what your mother says."

"Don't say that in front the viscountess unless you want to feel the barb of her tongue. She disliked him before his death and despised him afterwards. I remember hearing the arguments whenever he made it home. He almost pilfered away my grandfather's legacy."

"Your mother intimidated him. She was beautiful, awake on every suit, and more educated than your father. Sure, he went to university, but he learned more about gambling and horse racing than ledgers and economics." He sighed, his blue eyes thoughtful.

"I have no doubt on that count." Nate had no illusions when it came to his parent.

Both men were silent for a time while they ate. "You look more like him with each passing year. There are times when I swear it's him riding up the road. He had some good qualities, you know."

"Yes, he was quite skilled with the opposite sex and the bottle. I'm thankful our similarities are only physical." Nate's features hardened and he took another long pull of ale.

"It wasn't until after the wedding he turned to drink as a serious escape. We grew up together, you know. He spent more time in the village than he did on the grounds of Pendleton. Got more affection from my ma than his own family bein' the youngest son doesn't count for much. He had a generous heart too, I'll give him that." Maxwell locked a gaze on Nathaniel. "His allowance was often used for coal or some such when he was younger. 'Max,' he'd say, 'make sure the Ludlows stay warm. Heard their pig died so they may be short this winter.' He never took credit for those kind acts. You have more in common with him than you think."

Nate shook his head, wondering if the excess ale had loosened Maxwell's tongue. He'd never heard that story before. Then again, the steward had always defended the late viscount. "His one truly good deed was hiring you. He died leaving his title to a child and his widow neck high in debt and scandal. You had your hands full."

"Lady Pendleton did not always appreciate my input. She also didn't like you rubbing elbows with the villagers or being guided by a commoner." He tore off a hunk of the crusty bread and popped it in his mouth. "Fortunately, she didn't have much choice. I stayed on for practically nothing, and no able body with good references would have been interested in working for a pittance with an outcast family."

"Your service and loyalty will never be forgotten. Not many men would have stood by their word to a drunk and a spoiled boy."

"I have been repaid thrice-fold, my lord. I originally did it for your father and then..." Maxwell smiled, embarrassment reddening his face. "I'm as proud of you as if you were my own son. It's been a long road, but the properties are thriving, and your investments have doubled. That should help your sister along when Lady Pendleton takes her to London next season."

"Speaking of seasons, Mother is hinting I go to town with them and look for a wife. She made it sound like I'm buying a horse at Tattersall's. The mandatory heir, I suppose." Nate shrugged. "Am I ready for leg-shackles?"

"You will have your hands full with Mistress Hannah. She's a diamond of the first water, she is." He took a huge bite of mutton then waved his fork as he continued. "But you are coming to an age for a wife. Twenty and five is a good time to begin looking. Do the pretty, just don't be in a hurry."

The barmaid sashayed past them, a smile turning up her rosebud lips and an invitation in her eyes. "I wouldn't worry about that, Maxwell."

"How was business in Durham?" Lady Pendleton tapped her violet hand-painted fan. It thumped softly against the arm of the forest green brocade chair. "Shall we consider another investment in cloth?"

Nate grinned, his back to his mother as he poured a snifter of brandy. He swirled the amber liquid, watching it cling and sparkle against the beveled crystal while he considered his response. She should have been a born a man. Her mind was quick, and she had a head for numbers. He remembered the first time they opened the accounts after his father died. Such unladylike language coming from this stiff and proper viscountess.

"I think not. Glasgow and Manchester have a stronghold on the weaving industry at this point. But the rugs are turning quite a profit. Everyone wants an Axminster or one that resembles it. I'll increase the investment there and see what happens." He turned to find her staring out the window, her mind obviously somewhere else. Very uncharacteristic. "Or we could import some elephants from India. I hear they plow a field faster than oxen but they eat more."

"Yes, of course." Her folded fan now made a steady beat against her knee. "I'm sure that will be fine."

"Mother, what is it?" He sat down across from her and laid a hand on hers, stilling the soft tap of the fan's blonde horn sticks against her thin muslin. "It's not like you to be distracted."

"It's Hannah. I'm worried about finding an appropriate match in London next year. Will *his* escapades be remembered? What if—"

"Now you sound like my sister. What if, what if, what if? What if Napoleon rises again, invades England, and we must all learn French?" He sighed and sat back against the lush velvet of the loveseat. "No good will come from worrying over things we have no control over. My sister is lovely and educated with a generous dowry. I cannot see her being a wallflower. Besides, there have been dozens of scandals in the last dozen years. No one cares anymore."

"Yes. Yes, you are right. I was remembering my introduction into society." Her gaze strayed to the window again. "Such a wonderful and hopeful time for me but I remember one girl who was the object of scandal. I started to befriend her but Mama insisted I keep my distance. And then I was swept away..."

"Mother," he said, taking both her hands in his, "I will make sure whoever marries Hannah is beyond reproach. She will not fall to the same fate as you. I promise."

Lady Pendleton closed her eyes, a wistful smile on her face, and pushed a thin hand through her ash-blonde hair. The afternoon sun slanted across the room, emphasizing the emerging lines forming around her eyes and mouth. When she looked at him, tears shone in her intelligent brown eyes. "What life might have been like if your father had not battled the bottle."

Nate shrugged. It didn't matter. "It's water under the bridge now. We must look to the future, and it appears bright. Can we not be happy with that?"

"Of course," she agreed, one knuckle dabbing at the corner of her eye. "Pour me some claret, would you?"

He went to the side table and filled a glass with the deep red wine. "Gideon arrives this week. It will be good to see him again."

"Will he stay long?" She accepted the small cordial glass. "Now if he were to take an interest in Hannah, we would not need a season. We could avoid London altogether."

Nathaniel chuckled. Gideon had been a close companion since university. It had been his suggestion to invest in cloth. His father, the Earl of Stanfeld, owned a weaving factory in Glasgow. He owed his friend a great deal since those investments had brought the first profits to the account books. Shoving his sister at a man who was avoiding marriage would not be considered proper gratitude. "Let's not scare him off as soon as he crosses our threshold, hmm? Besides, he's as fond of her as a sister. I don't see that changing."

Supper was announced and he extended his arm to his mother. Her pale skin emphasized the dark circles under her eyes. Her usually erect shoulders drooped slightly, suggesting weariness. It could be just the progressing years but he doubted it. Perhaps he'd invite the physician for a visit when Gideon arrived. He'd been a good friend of the family since before his father had passed. Dr. Goodman could discreetly observe Lady Pendleton and request an examination if he felt it necessary. It would put Nate's mind at ease.

Nathaniel and Gideon galloped the horses across the meadow, jumped the hedge, and pulled up along the edge of a steep slope. They could see for miles at this vantage point, and the smell of freshly turned soil and pine wafted in the breeze. There hadn't been a moment of silence since his friend had arrived that morning. His mother and Hannah had commandeered poor Gideon before he'd wiped the dust off his boots.

Their friendship was a perfect example of opposites attracting. Nate's friendly, outgoing personality had opened up the serious and quiet nature of his friend. Gideon was dark with intense sapphire blue eyes. Nathaniel had his father's dark blond hair streaked by the sun and brown eyes flecked with gold. Together, they had accumulated a string of conquests. Both men enjoyed any outdoor activity, though again, Gideon preferred horses and fencing where Nathaniel had a reputation as a boxer and an excellent shot.

Both men dismounted, looking over the vibrant green fields dotted with white fluffy sheep. The horses quietly munched on spring grass, occasionally pricking their ears at an errant *baa* from below. Nate removed a small flask from his saddlebag, took a long pull, and wiped his mouth with his sleeve. He offered it to his friend, who did the same.

"I saw your hesitation when Mother asked about the earl. I know what you told them, but I know you too well. His condition has not improved, has it?"

Gideon shook his head. "No, I'm afraid not. He's bedridden at this point, and there doesn't seem much hope for recovery. But what is the point in worrying the women?"

"I'm deuced sorry to hear that. How are your mother and sisters?" Nate had always liked Lady Stanfeld. He'd always considered the Scottish beauty and the stodgy earl an odd couple. Yet they were devoted to each other.

"She is optimistic as always and refuses to believe he will die. Says he's too stubborn to give up, and the reaper would only send him back. Truth be told, I'm more concerned about her than of Father. He has suffered for months, and his breathing is more labored with each week. He told me the other day he was ready for death to come collect what was left of him." He let out a sigh in a loud rush. "I didn't have the heart to tell Mama."

Nate noticed the additional creases around his friend's mouth and deep blue eyes. It was hard to lose a parent at any age, especially if father and son were close. The vague recollections of his own father included much laughter, riding behind him on a great stallion to visit Maxwell, and playing Battledore and Shuttlecock on the lawn. These did not seem to fit the description of the man Mother had found so lacking.

"Now that I've taken over the duties of the earldom, I understand why you are so busy." Gideon took another swig from the flask and handed it across his saddle.

"Being in charge is not all bank notes and balls."

"No, indeed. So Pendleton, I was wondering..." Gideon ran a hand through his raven hair. He looked up to see the offered whiskey and took a drink before continuing. "My youngest sister has caused quite the scandal. Have the on-dits made it this far north?"

"Ha! As a matter of fact, yes, but I didn't want to bring it up. She's run off with some bastard of an Irish duke?"

His friend nodded. "The news revived my father for a bit. He found the energy to bluster and grumble. Wanted to hire a mercenary or two to go after her, but Mama convinced him otherwise. He seems a good enough fellow, though, and is able to support her in proper style."

"Your youngest sister was always a little hoyden—and my favorite, of course."

"Of course."

"On the subject of sisters, I should warn you. Mother may try to push Hannah in your path. I advised her against it but... Well, you know Lady Pendleton." Nate grinned. "Not that my sister would have a bracket-faced ne'er-do-well as yourself."

"Good God, she'd have my head on a pike the first time I tried to order her about. Much too independent for my taste. She'll be coming to market next year?" Gideon gave a snort. "I don't envy you that task. I've been through it with three sisters, and I'm thankful it's over."

"How long will you stay? Maxwell will want to have a bumper with you."

"Still mingling with the common folk? You really should try to distance yourself. Making friends with the villagers makes it that much harder if they can't pay their rent or hold out a hand for a charitable coin."

"They are people like you and me. And there *is* a difference between mingling and having some compassion. I make better decisions if I understand my tenants' positions. They don't take advantage of me, and I don't let them starve." The corner of his mouth quirked up. "It's economics, my friend. I'd think you'd understand that."

"Spoken as a true prodigy of Ezra Maxwell. Call it what you like but watch yourself. It's always better if they know their place. However, I do like your steward. He's a great gun and done well by you."

Nate scanned the outlying pastures and the one road leading through the countryside and into the village. An old woman hobbled along with a tall walking stick, a cloth bag slung over her shoulder. Even from this distance, he guessed it to be the old healer Mrs. Stanley collecting herbs. He gave her a quarterly allowance to tend to the poorer families in the village. The others paid her by coin or goods. Some of the tenants didn't like her coal-black eyes and thought her more a witch than a healer, but the closest physician was fifty miles away.

"How long did you say you were staying?" he asked, looking away from the road.

"A few days at the most. I'm on a business errand and headed to the weaving mill in Glasgow. My cousin wants to add cotton to the wool and flax production." Gideon waved a hand toward the sheep. "My father says we have the raw materials we need and importing cotton will be less profit and more risk. I'm going in his stead to get the details and make a decision."

"I'll never be able to thank you enough for advising on that investment in the cloth factory. It was the beginning of our family's return to society." If he were a demonstrative man, Nate would give this man a bear hug. "Anything I can do in return, remember I am always here."

"Stop! It's called friendship. I consider you one of the few men I can trust. Now, shall we go see what drink Maxwell has stored in the cupboard?" Gideon tossed the reins over his black gelding's neck. "If we are very lucky, his wife will have some fresh bread butter pudding. That woman can do miracles in that tiny kitchen."

"I'll race you to the top of the hill just above the village." Nate put a foot in the stirrup and then cursed as Gideon spurred his horse and took off. "You whey-faced scoundrel. Do you cheat at the tables too?" he yelled, jumping into the saddle and kicking his bay.

Nate gained on Gideon, who applied the crop to his horse and pulled ahead once again. Both men broke a sweat along with their mounts as they crested the hill. A black coach, pulled by two pairs of grays, trotted along the road below. The village of Pendle did not get many visitors, especially in a fine carriage. It carried no crest and wasn't the mail, so it poked Nate's curiosity. Were they lost? Or were they heading to Pendle Place?

Ahead of the unidentified coach, Old Mrs. Stanley was still making her way slowly home. As she approached a patch of woods, two young men emerged and approached her. Nate's eyes narrowed as he studied the duo. "Those two lads don't look familiar."

Mrs. Stanley flapped her hands at the newcomers and shook her head. The two males assumed a crouched position with their arms out at their sides and circled their prey, preventing escape. One man tried to grab her bag, and the feisty healer hit him on the head with her walking stick.

"Why those bloody footpads!" Nate dug his spurs into the gelding's flanks and tore down the hill, Gideon close on his heels.

As they galloped down the hill, the carriage pulled to a stop. One of the assailants fled while the other turned his attention to the new arrivals and pulled a pistol. A woman in a deep blue velvet cape and bonnet emerged from the coach. A shot rang out and the driver grabbed his shoulder, dropping his whip. The woman snatched it from the ground, picked up her skirts, and ran toward the ruffians. To his shock, the slight female raised her arm and flicked the whip, slashing the scoundrel until he dropped his weapon. The driver of the coach must have been in shock also for he sat frozen in his high seat.

"By Christ, an avenging angel," shouted Gideon from behind. "Who the devil is she?"

Nathaniel had no idea, but by God he would find out. He only hoped she didn't turn the whip on him.

"Anybody can become angry—that is easy, but to be angry with the right person and to the right degree and at the right time and for the right purpose, and in the right way—that is not within everybody's power and is not easy."

Aristotle

Chapter Four

Just Outside Durham, Northern England

Eliza stroked her daughter's dark curls. Althea's lips were pursed and moving in her sleep, a bit of spittle spreading a small dark stain on her mother's knee. The coach hit a rut, bumping its passengers into the air and back down on the cushioned bench.

"My lady, I really must know where we are bound. While it *is* exciting, stealing away at dawn like a spy, no one will know where to find me." Mrs. Watkins smiled but one hand gripped the leather strap dangling by her head, knuckles showing white. Her brown traveling dress and matching pelisse were dusty from days on minor country roads. She pushed a frizzy, fading auburn strand back under her bonnet and fanned her heaving chest with her other hand.

"I thought you had no family, which is one reason you were hired." Eliza heard the tone in her own voice, sharp and suspicious, and hated it. She was not a deceptive person by nature, nor did she appreciate adventure. But Falsbury had insisted that their destination be concealed. Besides, the woman would find out soon enough.

"I-It's not a family member, you see, only a friend. I don't want her to worry." This time her smile was genuine, making her blue eyes crinkle. "She has been very kind to me since I was a young lass."

Oh, botheration! The poor woman was a spinster with no living family, and she'd dragged her away from her companion. It didn't matter the situation was dire, Eliza did not need to be rude. It also occurred to her that she'd had no idea

"I do apologize, Mrs. Watkins. Lord Falsbury has us both at sixes and sevens. If you must correspond with anyone, please do not give our direction. Only let them know that you are in fine trim." She leaned across the carriage and squeezed the governess's hand. "It is imperative in order to keep Lady Althea safe."

The older woman covered her mouth, eyes large. "Oh, my lady, you know I would never do *anything* to harm my sweet Thea. It's not important at all, don't you fret about it."

"I hope to explain everything soon, and we can laugh about this covert escapade. But in the meantime, secrecy is of the utmost importance. There are very few people who know. Very few people the marquess or I trust."

Mrs. Watkins's chin shot up and a hand went to her bosom. "And I am one of those trusted employees?"

Eliza nodded, hiding the smile teasing her lips.

"I'll guard the little one with my life, I will. Nothing more need be said." The governess tipped her head and watched Althea sleeping. "I can't imagine anyone wanting to hurt such an angel as herself."

Eliza nodded again, leaned her head back against the stuffed velvet, and closed her eyes. Exhausted, she tried to empty her mind. They would reach Sunderland Castle today. The trip had been long since they avoided the major roads and tolls. After multiple nights at small out-of-the-way inns, she was ready for a comfortable bed with layers of ticks, filled with feathers and down. Last night, there had only been three mattresses—the first two stuffed with straw and the top one with flock. The rope across the frame had not been tightened in quite a while, and the whole bed sagged. Her back ached, her eyes burned from crying and lack of sleep, and her head pounded from multiple days in a jarring vehicle. The crunch of the wheels against the road and the sway of the coach finally lulled her to sleep.

It was so dark. She ran toward the tiny pinprick of light and the sound of wailing. Eliza ran and ran but her mother's voice never seemed any closer. "Where are you? I'm coming."

"You can't help her now. I've done her in, and this whining little chit is next."

Eliza kept running. Her lungs burned, and it took all her effort to move one leg then another. The blackness surrounded her like an opaque mist, swirling around her feet, clinging to her skin. Screaming, she stumbled and fell. A child whimpered and Eliza looked up to see a hulking shadow in the narrow ray of light. He held Althea high above his head with one hand.

"Obedient daughters incur less pain. Have you been obedient?"

She shook her head, a trembling hand reaching for her daughter. "I will, I will be obedient. I promise. Please don't hurt her."

"You will do as I say? No tricks?" He hissed the last word. "Let's be certain of this."

He dropped the child into the arms of the woman at his feet. With a sneer, he took a fistful of her hair and pulled Mama's head up. "Let me show you what will happen if you disobey again."

Her mother's empty eyes looked up, the dark circles giving her a face a ghostlike appearance. She handed the baby to Eliza. "Take care of my granddaughter. I will be out of my misery soon."

His fist came down, cracking a bone in her mother's face and snapping her head backwards. A small sob escaped but her eyes remained determined. She moved her head back and forth tentatively and worked her jaw. Slowly she stood and placed Althea in Eliza's trembling arms. "My life is over. Yours can be different. Don't give up. Don't give in to him."

This time his boot kicked her in the back, and she fell face forward. Her chest rattled as she took in a breath. Rising to her knees, she pleaded with Eliza, her words accompanied by a sickening wheeze. "Don't. Give. Up."

He buried his fingers in her dark matted hair and yanked hard. She closed her eyes, a tear *escaping down her battered face. In a hoarse whisper, she uttered her last word. "Promise me."*

"I promise, Mama. I promise." Eliza clutched Althea to her and backed away.

Her father's fist came down once more. Her mother crumpled to the ground. One gasp and her body stilled.

"NO! NO!"

"My lady, wake up. Please, you will frighten the child."

Eliza's eyes flew open, gasping as she drew in air. Althea squirmed on her lap, rubbing her eyes with chubby fists. Sunlight streamed through the window slats, and she pulled the cord, yanking them up to breathe the cool air, in then out. In then out. As her lungs filled again and again, her body relaxed. The trembling stopped. It had been a dream. Only a dream.

The carriage slowed and Eliza poked her head out to see what lay ahead. Two young men were circling an aged woman lying on the ground. She wore a white blouse and dusty gray skirt, a bag clutched beneath her. Her face, streaked with tears and dirt, scrunched up in anger.

"I won't give it up. You won't pinch my pocket, you jackanapes," she screeched at them as one kicked her in the ribs.

"Devil take it, keep the blasted weeds. We saw the farmer give you a purse, now hand it over."

"Bloody hell, leave that poor woman alone," yelled the driver.

"Let's get out of here. We don't need no more trouble for a few shillings," said one man.

"When we're about to be flush in the pocket?" Then he cursed as his partner escaped into the woods.

The carriage rolled to a stop, and the ruffian pulled out a flintlock pistol and pointed it at the driver. "Tell your passengers to remove themselves. And bring their purses and jewelry."

Watching the old woman curled around her burlap sack, something inside Eliza snapped like a twig. She handed Althea to Mrs. Watkins. "Don't move until I call for you." She opened the door and stepped out. Rage burned deep in her soul, and heat spread up her neck. With clenched fists trembling, she locked eyes with the footpad. He would not strike that poor thing again. She'd had enough of overbearing, malicious men.

"My lady, no, you mustn't," the governess cried, peeking out of the window.

"Do as I say." Eliza didn't recognize her own voice, the deadly control in it.

"Well, well, ain't this a honey-fall." The footpad grinned, showing blackened teeth. He swiped at his scruffy beard and spit off to the side. "Where is your purse, *my lady*?"

Eliza stopped next to the coachman's step and then everything happened in a blur. The driver spoke and bent toward her, the pistol fired and hit him in the shoulder. He howled in pain, clutching at his injury and dropping the whip.

Eliza's heart pounded as blood seeped between the coachman's fingers. She looked back at the ruffian. No longer concerned with the driver, the thief turned and walked back to the elderly woman. His hulking form, the sound of his voice, the fist clutched at his side...

"NO!" She grabbed the whip at her feet and charged the man. "Leave her be. The devil take you or I will!"

The whip cracked and slashed the man's back. He howled and froze as if in disbelief. Eliza watched the slow spread of red seep through his torn coat. Deliberately he turned, his arms out and face contorted. "You bitch, you'll pay for that."

She slashed out again before he could advance. And again. And again. She gained more strength with each blow, counting off the sins of her father.

Snap! "For Mama."

Snap! "For my childhood."

Snap! "For the kittens you drowned before my eyes."

Snap! "For my horse Thunder you rode to death."

Eliza heard a muffled cackle, a disjointed odd laughter as the man crouched low and covered his face with his hands. The moment seemed suspended, and nothing mattered but making this fiend pay. All motion slowed and sound was distorted as if she were under water. But her focus remained. Stop the evil before her.

"Don't. Give. Up."

The whip cracked. A scream of pain.

"Promise me."

"I p-promise"—the snap of leather, a hoarse male voice—"I promise w-whatever it is. P-please stop." Somewhere in the distance a child cried, hoofbeats hammered the ground.

Something caught her wrist, and she twisted, her other hand slapping and scratching at the force blocking her.

"Mama," called a small voice from far away. "Mamaaa."

Eliza blinked. *Althea*. Cheeks wet, chest heaving, a tremor racked her entire body. She looked into a strong face with a square jaw and soft brown eyes before the world went black.

Nathaniel yanked back on the reins and hit the ground before the horse slid to a stop. The woman stood panting, her feet wide apart, chest heaving, yelling with each flick of her wrist. He had caught only a word here or there on the wind, but her vehement tone had made him pause.

Kittens. Thunder. Promise. Damnation, the gel must be mad. He'd never seen a female fly into the boughs like this.

For a moment, she cast her attention on him as he strode toward her. Gideon had been correct. An avenging angel—with reddened eyes, a hauntingly beautiful tear-streaked face, and a determined set to her jaw. She'd lost her bonnet, and a thick straight mane of golden hair tumbled around her waist, swaying as she raised an arm to strike again.

Mrs. Stanley, still on the ground and clutching her burlap bag, hooted in vengeful glee with each smack of the whip. Gideon dismounted and approached the footpad from the rear, who now lay crouched in a ball against the onslaught. Nate came up behind the frantic woman and grabbed her wrist. The swirl of her deep blue traveling coat brushed his thighs, and he pulled her close to avoid being struck with the dangling leather.

She turned, the other hand coming up to slap his face. He squinted, tipping his head so his cheek took the brunt of it, and seized her other wrist to swing her around. She confronted him with violet eyes darkened by rage and locked her intense glare on his face. Nate's gaze traveled from the flushed cheeks to the creamy bosom, rising and falling as her breath came in short pants. A whiff of peppermint tickled his nostrils as she struggled for air. He lingered over the full quivering lips and wide unseeing eyes. Despite her anger and bravado with a whip, those lovely orbs held fear and desperation. And something else... Retribution? It tore at his soul like the frightened doe he'd found one summer surrounded by the neighbor's hounds, guarding her dead fawn against all odds.

When her fingers turned to claws, he pulled her close again. A child screamed for its mama, and the woman blinked, long pale lashes sparkling with tears. He wanted to scoop her up and murmur comforting words in her ear. Smooth the anxiety from her brow. Then fate granted his wish, and her legs gave way. He lifted her in his arms before her body slumped to the ground. A plump woman with a mess of graying auburn hair emerged from the carriage.

"My lady. Oh my poor mistress." She wiped her sweating forehead with a handkerchief, struggling to hold on to the toddler with her free hand. She lost the battle.

"Mama," the small girl cried as she yanked her wrist away and ran to Nate, tripping only once on the hem of her little sky blue frock.

"Wet go. She *my* mama. No hurt my mama." The little upstart pummeled his thigh with her fists. By God, if she didn't take after her mother.

"I'm saving her from the bad man, not causing her harm." The dead weight in his arms tossed her head against his chest and moaned softly. Without thought, his hold tightened around the limp form.

"Oh." The girl's fist stopped midair, and she tilted her head. "Mama good?"

Her bottom lip trembled and tears turned her huge round eyes indigo. She was a fetching little chit.

"Yes, my little hellion, Mama is good."

"I somehow feel you've got the better end of this bargain." Gideon held the torn and bleeding ruffian by the back of his coat collar, one arm pulled behind the attacker's back. "You're the hero, and I'm in need of a bath." Gideon's disheveled cravat carried the same dirt and traces of blood as his once-pristine white shirt and gray riding coat.

Nate ignored his friend and hid a grin as he turned to the traveling companion. "I am Viscount Pendleton, at your service. May I set your mistress inside the coach?"

She nodded. "She is Lady Eliza, the Dowager Countess of Sunderland, and her daughter Lady Althea."

"Relation of the Earl of Sunderland?" he asked. The earl's castle was only a long day's ride on a fast horse. Two by carriage.

"Yes, my lord. The earl is her brother-in-law."

She stepped aside, picked up Althea, and allowed him entry to the carriage. Nate ducked his head low, his chin perilously close to the lady's cleavage, and laid her gently across the seat. Peeling off his riding coat, he rolled it up and placed it gently beneath her head. Long lashes fluttered against her now pale cheeks.

So this must be Grace's cousin, the widow. Grace had lived at Boldon Estate and they'd grown up together. His family had attended her wedding when she married Christopher, the present Earl of Sunderland. He had tragically inherited the title when his twin brother fell from a horse and broke his neck, leaving behind a pregnant wife. This unconscious woman. He looked out at the curious little girl again. The child had her father's coloring and her mother's tenacity. The youngster had stopped her whimpering and now focused a curious stare on him.

He squatted beside Lady Sunderland and stroked her damp cheek to push away a wet blonde lock. The fury no longer hardened her features, giving her a completely contrary appearance. Her face now showed gentle breeding and a soft nature. She was a total conundrum. Fierce yet fragile, terrified yet valiant—and utterly stunning. Nate exited the carriage, his pulse racing.

"I must see to Mrs. Stanley," he explained with a nod of his head in the victim's direction.

It took a few minutes to get Mrs. Stanley on her feet and a complete retelling of the debacle. "My side will be sore and bruised but nothing broken," she assured Lord Pendleton. "Oh, that poor tortured soul. Did ye see those eyes, my lord? She's fighting demons of her own."

Gideon had tended the driver's shoulder. In turn, the coachman found a rope to tie the footpad's wrists and ankles. He now lay face down on the back of the carriage, securely fastened. His back was a crisscross of shredded wool, ripped skin and congealing blood.

"The coachman's pistol wound is superficial, and he says he's able to drive. But what will we do with that bloody cur?" asked Gideon, his tone telling Nate exactly what he'd *like* to do to him.

"We'll send for the constable. In the meantime, he can stay at the blacksmith's tied up to a post." Nate helped the governess, who identified herself as Mrs. Watkins, and little Althea into the carriage. This time, the child grinned at him. Her dark curls bounced as she climbed the steps one tiny foot at a time and gripped his fingers for balance.

"Me do myself." Althea took the last step then reached for a doll on the cushioned bench. She held it to her chest as the revived Lady Sunderland, now sitting up, lifted Althea onto her lap.

"I-I cannot thank you enough for rescuing us, sir," she said in a husky but strained voice. His angel smiled weakly and held out her hand. "I feel at a disadvantage, not knowing my rescuer."

"I am Lord Pendleton, and you fended off the villains on your own." He bowed. *How could this be the same woman who just beat a man to a pulp?* "I assume you are traveling to Sunderland Castle. May I suggest you stop at my home and freshen up after your ordeal? I am well acquainted with Lady Grace and will send word to Lord Sunderland that you have been delayed."

"You know my cousin?" Strength returned to her voice and now her smile was genuine. "It's been too long since I have seen her."

"Yes, our families are neighbors, and we played together since I was in a skeleton suit and she in short frocks."

Her lips turned up slightly at the mention of the childhood outfits. "Well, then we would appreciate your assistance very much."

"Would you mind if Mrs. Stanley rode along with you? She's the healer in our village. Perhaps the short ride will ease her concern for you, and she can thank you for your intervention. And after the treatment she's received, I'd rather she didn't walk."

"Of course, she is more than welcome."

"We need to stop and drop off the, er, damaged luggage in the back," he added as he handed Mrs. Stanley into the coach.

"And I hope that devil's son rots in hell after they hang 'im," the elderly woman added and spat at the vagabond. "Now, let me take a look at you, my lady."

"Really, I'm fine. You took the beating, not me."

"I admit I'm still a bit shaky. It takes a lot to ruffle my feathers, but those louts managed it." She sank onto the plush cushion and sighed.

"Well now, just sit back and catch your breath. Such courage you showed," said Mrs. Watkins in an awestruck tone. "I'd have handed over whatever the rascals wanted. Except my little mistress, here."

"As my husband used to say, every storm brings a rainbow. I haven't ridden in a fine carriage since I helped deliver Lord Pendleton and his sister." Mrs. Stanley winked at Lady Sunderland. "His father always sent the family coach, and I'd assist until the physician arrived." She shook her head. "You just never know what tomorrow will bring, now do ye?"

Nathaniel chuckled at the villager's philosophy. Fate definitely had a sense of humor. And if today was any indication, tomorrow promised to be quite another adventure.

> *"If adventures will not befall a young lady in her own village, she must seek them abroad."*
>
> Jane Austen, *Northanger Abbey*

Chapter Five

Pendle Place

Pish and perdition! Eliza pushed her back against the door. *What must they think of me?* Her throat thickened with mortification. The dream, the footpads, the whipping... Images of her father. The complete and resolute decision to fight back. What had come over her?

Fear. Yet fear made her cower, not take the lead against a man who could easily have overpowered her. It had been the surprise, of course. What male would expect a female of gentle birth to act like a derived banshee? Perhaps she had tendencies like her father.

No. Never. A smile played around the corners of Eliza's mouth. Had she said those things out loud? The thoughts spinning in her mind like a vortex while she took her anger out on that scoundrel? Mrs. Watkins had rambled on and on how she had flown to the old woman's rescue, grabbed the whip when the coachman was shot, and saved the day. Saved the day! She was no heroine, by any stretch of the imagination. Even now they were running from danger.

If Lord Pendleton had not intervened, Eliza might have... No, she couldn't think about it now. A lady's maid had set out one of her evening dresses, and a tub sat in front of the hearth, steam rising from the heated water. Yes, a good soak would help her think clearly. Althea was safe with Mrs. Watkins in the adjoining room. She could hear her daughter's high-pitched voice and the sound of splashing water.

Eliza peeled off her clothes and left them in a trail behind her. Stepping into the tub, she lowered herself with an audible sigh. How fortunate to come across friends of Grace. Lady Pendleton had insisted they stay the night. Her wish for a decent bed had been granted by a twist of fate. She'd heard so much about Grace's neighbors and Pendle Place over the years, and now she was here.

As a girl, she and her mother had visited Boldon Estate once a year. It was always an escape that ended too soon. Then Lord Boldon had loaned her father a substantial sum. Lady Boldon, with the permission of Lord Boldon, had used the transaction to make a bargain with her brother-in-law and finagle more time with her sister and niece. The debt would be considered paid in full under one condition. Eliza and her mother were allowed two visits a year to Boldon and added an annual trip to London. This provided the women an opportunity to shop, see the sights, and introduce Eliza to the city and society ways.

The heat of the bath worked its wonders, and she was relaxed enough to take in her surroundings.

The room was tastefully decorated with pastels of peach and green silk paper covering the walls. The huge bed had ornately carved rails of walnut and fringed peach curtains hung from a brass ring in the ceiling, forming a luxurious tent over the frame. A green counterpane with tiny ivory and peach roses embroidered along the edges covered the mattresses. Eliza knew the second she lay upon the mountain of down and feathers, sleep would claim her.

Instead, she soaked the tension from her muscles, the scent of lavender easing her lids closed. The image of her rescuer floated before her. A handsome man, so different from her husband. Lord Pendleton's frame was shorter, more muscular and sturdy than Carson's slight but taller build. He had taken off his riding jacket to cushion her head. His strong arms had strained through the thin material of his shirt. But his eyes had claimed her attention. Such kindness in those soft brandy-colored eyes, the afternoon light adding glints of gold that had quite taken her breath away.

She wasn't nervous around this man, though he made butterflies take flight in her stomach. Grace's description of him had not included how handsome he was or how charitable. He had been her cousin's best friend next to her. She remembered Grace's letter, telling of the viscount's death, and how Nathaniel had leaned on her. Then the tables had turned when Grace's mother had died. Her "beloved Nate" she had called him. He had swooped in to lift her spirits each time she was at her wit's end caring for an infant brother and a bereaved father. After Grace's mother died, the trips to London had stopped but the visits to Boldon Estate had mercifully continued.

Eliza rose and dried herself off. Life at Landonshire Manor had made her quite adept at taking care of her daily toilette. The marquess had not appreciated witnesses to his temper, and a lady's maid had been hard to keep. Instead, she and her mother had assisted each other when necessary and could easily attend themselves unless formal evening dress was demanded. Those occasions had been rare. She'd only attended one ball before going to London to meet her betrothed. One couldn't really call that a season since her marriage had already been arranged.

She remembered her mother's joy at the wedding. Had it been the glitter of the wedding celebration or the reprieve from her husband's temper? Either way, it had been two weeks of bliss for both of them. Lunches in their honor, dances in the evenings, all culminating to the marriage ceremony. Eliza had seen what other girls' lives were like, carefree with constant activity. She remembered their whines and complaints of the doldrums when they were forced to sit through another afternoon visit with their mothers. Oh, to have had a life of boredom instead of constant angst and punishment.

Self-pity achieves nothing. Make yourself presentable and prove to the Pendletons that you are not a heathen. Donning a pale rose muslin gown with an overlay of ivory lace, she combed her hair and deftly arranged it high on her head. She pulled several strands out to fall against her neck then used her finger to wrap the locks into an illusion of curls. The delicate waves of gold brushed her cheeks as she slipped on her ivory kid slippers, the points sticking out just beneath her scalloped hem. She would check on Althea and then go down to properly meet her hosts.

Next door, the adjoining room looked as if a storm had hit. Althea's clothes had been pulled from her trunk and strewn about the furniture. The rug in front of the hearth was wet, and a towel hung from the mantel, drying in front of the burning coals. A small head, eyes closed and damp curls clinging to her face and neck, lay on the wrong end of the couch. A blanket had been pulled over her narrow shoulders, and she slept with the abandon of one who had nothing to fear.

Eliza meant to keep it that way.

She took a deep breath. This child was her life. To see her so peaceful, with no worries except finding her favorite toy, filled Eliza's heart with happiness and relief. Her daughter's life would be different.

"Oh, Lady Sunderland, my apologies," said Mrs. Watkins as she hurried around the room collecting the clothes. "She needed to run after being cooped up so long. We played a game—"

"No need to explain, I know my daughter." Eliza smiled to reassure the governess. "I've plucked you from your bed to a coach, forced you to swear secrecy on our whereabouts, and subjected you to bully ruffians who might have killed us. You are a saint, Mrs. Watkins, and my saving grace. Please accept my sincerest gratitude."

The woman blushed, her dimples deepening. "Why thank you, my lady. We were in the suds today, weren't we? But it does my heart good to hear such words of praise from a fine lady as yourself."

"And I thank *you* for being so patient and understanding."

Mrs. Watkins flapped a plump hand at her. "It's just my way. Now you go downstairs, forget all about this afternoon's hubble bubble, and enjoy a fine evening. That Lord Pendleton is a fine-looking gentleman"—she winked at her mistress—"and he'll take your mind off your troubles if you let him."

Eliza left with a lighter heart. As she descended the stairs, the sound of deep laughter drifted from the parlor. It set wings off low in her belly. The viscount just might be a distraction from her present troubles. And lead her into another kind of danger.

"Nathaniel, this sounds like one of those ridiculous romance novel where the adventurous, independent heroine wins the day." Lady Pendleton frowned, her fan once again tapping against her lap. "You say she beat him with a whip? Gracious! Grace always spoke of her as a timid thing."

"There was nothing timid about her this afternoon. But once I stopped her, she fell apart and fainted dead away. I had to carry her into the coach." Nate remembered the warmth of her body next to his and the smooth silkiness of her hair feathered against his neck. *Enough or you'll embarrass yourself in front of your mother!* "It was almost like she was another person once she came to."

"Perhaps she's one of those defenders of the weak and unfortunate, like your father." Lady Pendleton said the last word with a curled lip. "Or there are windmills in her head. Well, we won't mention it unless Lady Sunderland brings it up first. I don't want to embarrass her."

"If she's skilled with a whip, I'd like to bring her along to London with us. It would be nice to have a champion with a weapon as deadly as Mother's sharp tongue." Hannah smirked and gave her brother a side glance. "Especially since she's been a bit smoky lately."

"On the first count, court holy water will get you nowhere, my dear child," her mother retorted with a smirk. "For the second, I'm distracted, that's all. My mind is as sharp as ever."

He let out a guffaw. "Only you would take that as a compliment. Your wit can be quite barbed, Mother. I agree with you on the other account though. Let's not discuss the earlier incident."

"Where is Gideon?" asked Hannah, changing the subject with a studied air of indifference, though her childhood crush was no secret. She picked at the beige sawtooth trim on the sleeve of her pale yellow muslin. "Did she scare him off?"

"Of course not, he's made of stronger stuff than that. Since I plan on escorting Lady Sunderland the rest of her journey, he decided to continue his trip to Scotland." He noted the flash of disappointment on his sister's face. "He promised to try to stop by for a few days on his way home. I'll invite the Dr. Goodman for a visit when Gideon returns."

"That's a wonderful idea. Perhaps we'll include the Sunderlands and Lord Boldon. Young Samuel must be nine or ten by now, perhaps old enough to come along for a picnic. The dowager countess has a daughter also, does she not?" Nate's mother stopped rapping her fan, her gaze fixed on the doorway. "Good evening, my dear."

Nate turned to find a vision of loveliness meeting his gaze. Her pale blonde hair was pulled up with ringlets caressing her pink cheeks. The rose and lace gown clung to her curves and the bodice dipped low, revealing a smooth creamy bosom. His face heated. The pulse in his neck took off like a fox in a hunt. Suddenly he was a schoolboy, fawning over his first infatuation. Except this was far from his first infatuation—or first anything. She could stir his blood with a look. He took one step forward, his hand held out in welcome.

"Lady Sunderland, may I introduce you?" He held out his arm and her hand rested lightly on his arm. A surge of warmth shot from her fingertips through his core. "This..." Violet eyes—no deep blue?—mesmerized him. His sight flickered back and forth from her smiling full lips to those indigo orbs.

"This is your mother, Viscountess Pendleton?" she asked, amusement in her tone.

Her soft, throaty voice made him wish they were alone in a dark garden. "Er, yes. Mother, may I introduce Lady Sunderland?"

His mother nodded.

"And my sister Lady Hannah."

His sister pushed back a stray strand of her dark honey-colored hair and moved forward with her arms open. "We are so thankful you are safe and all ended well."

Nate shot Hannah a look. Hadn't they just agreed not to bring it up? His sister only grinned. He realized she'd just pulled him from a bumble bath and saved him from looking like a Johnny Raw. Back in control, he escorted Lady Sunderland to a chair.

"As am I. The excitement had my Althea done to a thumb, and she's sound asleep. My utmost gratitude for your kind hospitality. I must admit, it's been quite a day." She smiled and nodded in return. "Please, call me Lady Eliza. I've reverted to my previous title since it can be quite confusing with my cousin now married to the earl."

"Well then, Lady Eliza, would you care for a cordial?" he asked, more comfortable being on neutral ground. "Supper should be announced shortly."

"After today, a glass of claret would not be out of order." She accepted the small crystal glass. "This is a lovely manor from what I've seen."

"Thank you. Perhaps Nathaniel would take you around the gardens after supper. They are beautiful even at night." Lady Pendleton smiled, a gleam in her eye.

Dash it! His mother had also noted his reaction to Lady Eliza. Thank God he would take her to Sunderland Castle tomorrow. He didn't trust his mother when it came to the parson's trap. Nathaniel was not unwilling to marry, but he had become accustomed to the idea of waiting until Hannah's season. Another year and he would indeed be ready.

But Christ, his own body betrayed him when she barely touched him. From Grace's babble about her cousin, he'd never expected such an exquisite creature. Distance. Yes, distance was just the thing.

Hannah moved to the side table and poured a glass of wine. "Will you be staying long with Grace?"

"I-I don't know. It has been three months since our last visit, so I'm certainly in no hurry to leave." She sipped at the claret.

Nate stared at the tiny drop of ruby red liquid on her top lip. Her tongue darted out to catch it just as their eyes locked. A becoming blush rose up her neck at the same time heat claimed his face.

"We've sent a brief explanation to Sunderland that you are here. Given the circumstances, I shall accompany you on the last leg of your journey." That delectable mouth curved up. Why was he so delighted the statement pleased her?

"I would hate to impose, my lord," she said quietly, eyes cast down now. "We have already put you out."

"Nonsense." Lady Pendleton's fan was tapping again. "My son would not rest well until he knew you were safely delivered. And Grace would have his head on a platter."

"Whatever you think is best, my lord." She peeked at him from under her thick pale lashes. "I admit the protection would be appreciated, especially with my young daughter traveling with me."

"It's settled then." He poured himself another glass of brandy and smiled to himself. This puzzle of a woman would be out of his system by the time he returned.

But it wasn't to be. The next morning, two letters arrived with the Sunderland seal. One to Nate from Kit, Lord Sunderland. The other to Lady Eliza from Grace.

Nathaniel,

We will arrive at Pendle Place this afternoon. I hope it is not an imposition to put us up for a night. There is a delicate matter we need to discuss with you concerning Lady Eliza. Afterward, I will escort her if necessary.

Sunderland

Short and to the point, as always. Odd. A delicate matter? What did Kit mean by "if necessary," he wondered, the image of the flaxen-haired hellcat, whip in hand, crowding his brain. Perhaps this beautiful creature was a shilling shy of a pound.

"Time will explain."
Jane Austen, *Persuasion*

Chapter Six

Eliza stared at the red wax insignia. This could not be good news. She slid a manicured nail under the seal. Grace's elegant slant filled the page.

My dearest Eliza,

My heart goes out to you. Not only are you sent scurrying across the country but you are accosted along the way. I thank the good Lord that Nathaniel stumbled across your path. Kit and I have discussed the situation, and he fears it is not safe for you here. But I have come up with a plan. We will come to you and enlist the aid of these dear family friends.

Please do not fret. Rest assured you are in the best of hands. You have both heard enough about the other to almost be old friends. I would trust Lord Pendleton with my own life. Give Althea a hug for me and I will see you soon.

Your loving cousin,

Grace

No! Her stomach churned at the thought of her shameful past coming to light in front of strangers. How could she face these people every day if they knew of her father's depravity—and her cowardice? Eliza gritted her teeth, determined to convince her cousin otherwise. In the meantime, she would not have the lady's maid unpack, in case she was successful. Though her stalwart cousin was rarely thwarted. Besides, Kit had every reason to worry over his wife's safety. Why should she endanger Grace? She couldn't, so Eliza could go along with their plan or give in to her father's demands.

Staying in close vicinity of the handsome viscount both excited and disturbed her. He would pity her or despise her. Either would be horrid. And the thought of her father finding her here, and the possibility of putting strangers, innocent people in harm's way... She blinked back the tears.

Deep breath. Deep breath. Where was that intrepid woman who saved the poor old lady yesterday? *In her right mind again!*

Althea burst into the room, Mrs. Watkins waddling behind her, mopping at her forehead with a handkerchief. The little girl flew onto the bed in a whirl of pink and gray, her dark curls bouncing.

"I won. I won. Miz Watins too swow." She giggled, balancing precariously from knees to feet, then jumped up and down on the mattresses.

"Gah! I'll remember not to say the word 'race' until I'm closer next time." The governess laughed and tucked her handkerchief into her bosom. "Gracious but she's quick."

"C'mon!" Althea cried as she fell on her bottom, wobbled to a standing position, and began again with a squeal. "Pway wif me, Mama. Jump, Miz Watins."

"My dear, I'm afraid the ropes wouldn't hold if we were to try that!" Eliza caught her daughter in midair and squeezed her tight. "I love you sooo much!"

"I wuv you mo'." She wrapped her arms around her mother's neck and gave her a sloppy kiss on the cheek. "Me hungwy."

"Mrs. Watkins, I'm afraid there may be a change in the itinerary. It seems my cousin and brother-in-law will arrive here this afternoon." Eliza arranged a smile on her face. "I'm not sure if we shall leave today or postpone our trip."

"Yes, my lady. It makes no difference to us. This child is easily entertained wherever we go." She took back her charge, set her on the ground, and firmly clasped her hand. "The garden may be a good place for this young one after breakfast. Let her run some and perhaps she'll take a nice nap this afternoon."

"That's a grand idea. I might join you. The fresh air would do me good."

"Come along, dear one. Don't get under that bed, I can't reach you there." Mrs. Watkins hurried after Althea, who had darted into the other room. Her voice faded as the door clicked closed. "Now where is that frock with the long ribbons? I can keep you close with those..."

With a quick check in the mirror, Eliza smoothed back her hair and gave another quick finger curl to her side locks. The dark blue of her traveling pelisse made her eyes appear a deeper blue. When she took it off, the purple muslin and lavender

trim and waistband of her gown brought out a violet hue. She'd always hated her eyes until Carson had complimented them. She'd considered them a peculiar color while he had called them remarkable. *My dear Carson. I miss our talks already.*

She headed down the stairs, hoping—no praying—that Lord Pendleton had also been informed of the alternate arrangement. It would give her more time to prepare herself for the gathering this afternoon. Knowing Grace, she did have a plan and good reasons for the change. Once again, she'd have to trust her cousin.

Nate watched his guest descend the stairs. If she was a bit touched, it didn't diminish her beauty. She caught his staring and gave him a bright but uncertain smile.

"It seems you must stay here a while longer," he said as he met her on the bottom step. "I hope you are not too disappointed. I am on my way to the breakfast room. Would you like to join me?"

Panic flared in her eyes. His jaw clenched at being the cause of it. Was she not comfortable here or was there something else? He had the distinct feeling there was much more to this young widow than she let on. What secrets did she hide? He wished Gideon were still here for he could always figure a person out. Always knew if they spoke the truth, only part of it, or told a Banbury tale.

"Does your mother know that I-we are not leaving immediately?"

"Yes, I was with them when I read the letter from Sunderland." He watched the relief brighten her eyes before they focused on her boots.

His mother could be intimidating, but supper last night had not been awkward. Except when Mother had spoken of her hope for grandchildren and asked if her parents doted on Althea. There had been an uncomfortable silence and then she'd mumbled about her father being busy and her mother disliking travel. Hannah covered the clumsy moment with an elaborate sneeze then changed the subject to the weather.

"A cup of tea does sound very good. I'm not sure if I could eat."

"Let's find out, shall we? Cook makes an excellent biscuit with a crispy top and fluffy middle. I'd have run away from home several times as a boy if it weren't for those biscuits." He warmed at the sound of her laughter. "Hannah cannot wait for Grace to arrive. We had a particularly wicked winter with little socializing. If she has her way, it will be a week-long house party."

"Hannah is lovely. Why has she not had a season yet?" Nate's pulse kicked up as she placed her hand on his arm. Moving down the hall, he considered how to answer that. How much did she know of his family's history? "Mother insisted she wait until eighteen. She was in a hurry to lose her only daughter."

"I can understand that," Lady Eliza agreed softly. "Hannah will be snapped up at the first ball."

"Not until I have interviewed and thoroughly terrified every suitor." He winked. "Only the strongest and most eligible will survive."

She gave a throaty chuckle as they entered the morning room. "How wonderful it must be to have an older brother."

"Hmph! I beg to differ," said Hannah from the dining table, brown eyes sparkling with mischief. "His motives aren't as altruistic as you think. He's afraid Mother will make him escort her to afternoon teas and join him when the neighboring ladies visit."

Nate gave an exaggerated shudder. "Run me through now and save me from such a fate."

"I'll send you off to a worse one, you impudent boy." Lady Pendleton waved a butter knife at him. "Lady Eliza, good morning to you. Please ignore my son's waggling tongue. Men, as you know, never mature in some aspects."

With a hand over his heart, Nate bowed. "I give in as I am outnumbered."

He pulled out a chair for Lady Eliza and watched her backside settle on the embroidered cushion. Hannah smirked at him. Sending her a warning glare, he proceeded to the side table and filled his plate with a rasher of bacon, eggs, and several biscuits.

"Would you like to try one?" He offered her the plate of biscuits.

"After your marvelous recommendation, how could I not?" She took one and slathered one half with creamy white butter. "Oh, my. These are delicious."

"Here, put some marmalade on it," he said around a mouthful. "If these aren't in heaven..." He stopped chewing as he watched her pile on the sweet preserves and lick off a chunk as it dropped onto her thumb. A throbbing began low in his belly.

What the hell is wrong with me?

"I wonder how Grace is coming on the repairs to the rest of the castle? The living quarters and main hall are so tastefully done." Lady Pendleton poured more tea and added a dollop of cream. "The place was in shambles when they moved in. I don't know how she did it."

"My cousin is very organized and industrious." Her lips turned up. "In other words, she can't stand to be idle."

"She always has a plan. Been that way since childhood. We never played a game or organized a party without a second scheme, in case something went awry." Nate snorted.

"It's saved our skins more than once. Remember the picnic by the stream?" asked Hannah. "The wind blew up a terrible storm, and we only had time to make it to that old woodcutter's cabin."

"On my property, and I didn't even it know it existed," continued Nate, "but there it was with blankets and a pile of wood and books!"

"Books?" Lady Pendleton stopped the last bite of biscuit midway to her mouth. "She'd stocked an old hut with books?"

"It seems Grace likes to read when she's stranded somewhere. So I made a fire, we spread a dusty but dry blanket on the floor, and Hannah read to us. One of those terrible romance novels females seem to adore." Nate rolled his eyes. "How can a flesh and blood male compare to the heroes in those books?"

"Quite impossible," agreed Lady Eliza. "When I was a young girl, they were my only escape. I used to..." The smile faded from her lips along with her voice. She sipped her tea, suddenly fascinated with the lace pattern of the tablecloth.

He studied her. What had caused that abrupt withdrawal? Yesterday an avenging angel and today a wounded doe. An unexpected urge to protect this woman rose in his chest. He hastened to cover the silence and his mother and sister's curious looks. "Between the fictional gallants and her own father, Lord Boldon was surprised any man passed muster with his daughter."

"Lord Sunderland is not just any man," she almost whispered.

"No, indeed he is not," agreed Nate. Something about her demeanor, the wistfulness in her tone roused him, and he found himself wanting to be "not just any man" in her eyes.

After a final cup of tea, coffee for Nathaniel, the ladies dispersed. He stopped Lady Eliza in the hall, not ready to leave her side yet. "What are your plans for the rest of the morning?"

"I'm joining Mrs. Watkins and Althea for a walk in the gardens. If you don't mind, that is." Lady Eliza smoothed an invisible wrinkle from her lilac dress, not meeting his eyes. "The sun has come out, and it's such a lovely day.

"I don't mind under one condition." He put on his most charming smile and was rewarded with the arch of one blonde brow. "You allow me to accompany such a lovely trio."

"We'd be delighted." She picked up her skirts and hurried up the stairs.

Nate rubbed his jaw as he watched her go, something about her behavior niggling the back of his brain. She was perplexing, but he no longer wondered about her sanity. He had a few questions for Sunderland—and hoped he was wrong about the answers.

"Let none think to fly the danger for soon or late love is his own avenger."

Lord Byron

Chapter Seven

Pendle Place
County Durham

Eliza hugged herself as the carriage approached. She could hear the crunch of wheels on gravel through the thick-paned glass of her bedroom. Her stomach flipped from both the excitement of seeing Grace and Kit again and anxiety of the discussion to come.

"Mama, Mama," cried Althea, running from the next room, doll hugged to her chest. "Dey coming! Dey coming!"

Grace had given the toddler a portrait of her and Kit inside a tiny heart-shaped locket. It was a way for the little girl to remember her since they could not visit as often as they'd like. Althea had lovingly placed it on her new doll. She climbed up onto the window seat, her face pressed to the pane, giggling as her breath steamed the glass.

"Shall we go down and greet them?" Eliza held out her hand, and the two headed for the stairs.

Mrs. Watkins hurried from the adjoining room. "I'm coming, my lady. I had to put the dominoes away. She loves lining them up and watching them fall."

"I know my cousin will want to spend time with Thea. As soon as they get settled, you may have some time to yourself." She smiled at the governess. "I'm afraid your day off came and went. You deserve to recuperate from this rambunctious child and replenish your patience."

"Oh, my lady, I do appreciate it, though I love her like my own. These are extenuating circumstances, and I don't mind a bit. But a leisurely walk without chasing the little mistress would be just the thing." She smoothed back her frizzy curls and her dimples deepened. "I've been eyeing those stables. You know how I love horses."

"It's settled then. After her nap, you may take the rest of the afternoon off. Perhaps Lord Pendleton could have someone introduce you to the head groom." Grace heard the commotion of happy voices outside as the carriage pulled up. She looked down at Althea, now pulling at her mother's hand with a grunt. "Stay beside me. I don't want you getting underfoot and stepped on by people or horses."

"Pwomise," Althea said and continued pulling.

Eliza reached the door as Grace gave Lord Pendleton an affectionate embrace. Her auburn hair was streaked with red and gold, her cheeks pink with pleasure.

"It's so good to see you!" she cried then hugged Lady Pendleton and Lady Hannah in turn. "I've been champing at the bit for spring. February was a terrible month for travel, and we were in the middle of another renovation in March.

Kit stood back, a patient but droll look in his black eyes. His dark looks, which the twins had inherited from their mother, always reminded Eliza of Carson. At first, he had been a constant reminder of what she had lost. Then Grace had pointed out that Althea would always know what her papa had looked like. Over time, seeing him became a reminder that some change could bring joy. Until her father had emerged from the depths of hell again.

"Auntie Gwace! Auntie Gwace!" Althea ran to Lady Sunderland and threw her arms around her knees.

The woman picked her up, squeezing her tightly. "Oh, how I've missed you. Did you get my letters?"

The girl nodded and leaned back, presenting her latest toy. "I have supwise fo' you." She held out the doll wearing the locket.

"Oh, my. What a lovely girl. She looks just like someone I know." Grace put a finger to her lips and tapped her foot. "Hmm, who is it she reminds me of?"

"She me! I name her Gwace!"

"I'm honored, Thea. And I see she has our locket." Grace fingered the necklace, a wistfulness showing in her eyes, and squeezed her again.

Eliza's heart went out to her cousin. She'd had a miscarriage the previous year. The physician had said there was no reason they would not have many more children, but so far Grace had not conceived again. In the meantime, she doted on Althea, who was now wiggling to get down. As soon as her feet hit the ground, the toddler headed full speed toward Kit and launched into his arms. The Earl of Sunderland caught her with a soft *oomph*.

"How is my beautiful lass, hmm?" he asked, kissing the top of her bouncing head. Then she threw her chubby arms around his neck and kissed him loudly on the cheek. "I didn't get quite get that answer. Could you tell me again?"

Althea laughed, grabbed his face between her two small hands, and gave him a kiss on the other cheek. "You miss me, UnKit."

He chuckled at her moniker, a cross between uncle and Kit. "Of course I do! Who is my favorite girl?"

"Me! Fo'ever me!" She squealed as he threw her up in the air and caught her.

"Again!"

Kit threw his yelping bundle in the air again, her frock puffing out like an umbrella. On the third landing, he placed her on his shoulders and headed toward the steps. "Up we go, Thea!"

Grace turned to Eliza and held out her arms. "My dear, sweet cousin." They hugged in silence and then Grace took Eliza's arm and whispered, "Trust me."

Kit and Althea led the rest of the group into the house, her small hands clutching Kit's chin like a death bandage. Inside the drawing room, he took her from his shoulders in a dramatic front flip and set her on his lap. He rubbed at the imprint of tiny fingernails under his chin. "There's a literal interpretation of a female getting her claws into a man."

Lord Pendleton chuckled. "Indeed, they do start young, don't they?"

Lady Hannah rolled her eyes. "How was your journey? Uneventful I hope."

"Yes, we started out early and stopped in the village to check on Mrs. Stanley." Grace's eyes grew serious. "The poor woman is lucky none of her ribs were broken."

"I stopped by the blacksmith. He's keeping a close eye on the footpad and says he's getting him acclimated for where he's going. Has him tied next to the kiln." Kit's concerned gaze fell on Eliza. "And how are you, sweet sister-in-law?"

Avoiding the question, she turned to the governess. "Mrs. Watkins, would you take Althea up for her nap? She may be hungry since she was too excited to eat this morning."

"Of course, my lady." She held out her hand to the child. "Are you hungry, my sweet?"

Althea nodded her head, dark curls bouncing. "Ginbwead, pwease."

"Gingerbread it is, and then a bit of a rest." She waited patiently while the girl gave her mother, aunt, and uncle a kiss and the rest a wobbly curtsy.

Silence prevailed until their footsteps faded down the hall.

Kit cleared his throat. "I'd like to thank you for your help in this matter."

"What exactly is the 'matter'? Your note was brief." Lord Pendleton took a seat on a tapestry-covered chair. "I assume there is more to this matter than the incident on the road."

Grace looked at Eliza and then Kit. "My cousin's father is... Let's say he enjoys inflicting pain in others. I was relieved when Eliza married Kit's brother and escaped his abuse. It seemed she was finally safe from harm."

Heat engulfed Eliza's face. She could not look up as Grace explained the situation. Would they judge her, pity her, or refuse to help her? With Sunderland Castle no longer an option, she truly would have to sail for America or marry that vile old man. Alone in a strange land or life with a lecher without her daughter. *Deep breath in. And out. Deep breath in. And out.* She focused on her breathing to keep the panic at bay as Lady Falsbury had taught her.

"So her father threatened Lady Eliza's mother and that darling little girl upstairs if she did not marry a common merchant?" Lord Pendleton asked. "That blasted cutthroat."

His mother shook her head. "Abhorrent behavior. But if he thinks she's somewhere on the Atlantic, why isn't she safe at Sunderland Castle?"

"Landonshire is no fool and neither is his partner. They'll put men sniffing around the docks. My father padded the wharfinger's pocket well to remember a young woman and child boarding a ship. But if he's offered more, who knows?" Kit shrugged his shoulders. "We don't want to take that chance until we have an alternative plan."

Eliza found her voice. "My brother-in-law cannot put his wife in danger. They have already done so much for me."

"No, that's not the reason," cried Grace. "I know your father. If he finds out you have not left the country, he'll send spies to the castle and Boldon. It's for your safety and Thea's, not ours."

Eliza blinked back the tears as Grace rose and put comforting arms around her. She would not cry.

"As you can see," Kit continued, "we need a place unknown to Landonshire. It seems fate has stepped in."

Looking at her hosts, Eliza apologized. "I am so sorry for this horrid affair. Please do not feel obligated to protect me. I am no relation to you and I would understand—"

"NO!" The word resounded against the brown and gold silk-covered walls.

Eliza cringed and blinked back tears at the harsh tone. She looked into the angry face of Lord Pendleton, her worst fear realized as she saw the disgust in his brandy-colored eyes flashing with gold.

"Of course, my lord," she said barely above a whisper, eyes downcast. "We did not unpack our trunks yet and can leave immediately." Her mind scrambled for her next move. "I appreciate everything you have done for us."

Pendleton issued a mumbled curse and then his boots appeared in her line of vision. A finger touched her chin and lifted her face.

"Forgive me, Lady Eliza, for my temper. You misunderstand." He gave her a half smile and bent on one knee. "I will gladly play your champion. I meant no to you leaving."

With his face so close to hers and treating her with such gentleness, she felt dizzy. Her eyes burned and she blinked again, determined to be strong and deserve this kindness. "Thank you," she whispered.

Nathaniel cursed when he saw Lady Eliza flinch. Sunderland had just explained her childhood had been filled with violence, and then he shouted. In anger. The image of anyone beating her, let alone her own father, enraged him. That strange protectiveness had spread through him again, and he wanted to shield her as he would his mother or sister or Grace. Only not *quite* the same.

He would have to be more considerate in the days to come. For she would stay under his roof as long as needed. His mother approached and gripped his shoulder. Nate stood, one hand covering hers.

"My dear, we would never turn you away. Even if Landonshire found you here, he would not harm myself or Hannah. As Lord Sunderland said, he is not a fool." She smiled. "Please, let us think of this as a house party."

Hannah joined in. "Oh yes! Grace, must you return right away? Stay for a week. We could have such fun."

Nate silently thanked his family. Lady Eliza's shoulders relaxed and a tremulous smile brightened her face. He looked into those shining violet eyes, her lashes dark with tears, and his mouth went dry. She was breathtaking. By God, he'd transform this timid creature back into the avenging angel he'd met the day before.

"Not to spoil the moment," Kit interrupted, "but we still don't have a solution. And I can see by my wife's adorable glare that we'll have a week to come up with a plan. She is rather good at that, you know."

"Eliza would be much more comfortable with the arrangement if we stayed for a bit," Grace agreed. "Lord and Lady Falsbury won't be in London for a few days. Even if Landonshire doesn't believe the story, we have some time before he makes his way to Sunderland or my father's estate of Boldon."

"It's settled then." Hannah clapped her hands. "Oh, we'll have a picnic on the river bank, ride..."

Nate's mind tuned out his sister's list. He watched the flurry of emotions crossing Lady Eliza's lovely face. Something about her drew him, and it was more than her beauty. He wanted to peel away the layers of doubt and fear and find the woman he had glimpsed. But first he must gain her trust. It would be work. She would be wary and resist, he was certain. Taking honey from a bee was a difficult task, yet the beekeeper was rewarded thrice-fold for the effort.

A movement beside him stopped his reverie. Grace took his arm and leaned into him, a brilliant smile sparkling in her clear green eyes. *Damnation!* Another female had caught his look. Was he so transparent?

She kissed his cheek. "You're wonderful, you know. Thank you. Eliza is my dearest friend."

Kit snorted. "Pardon me but I believe this whole plot was *my* idea."

Giggling, Grace returned to her husband and gave him a chaste kiss on the lips. "You already know I think you're wonderful."

A teacup clattered against a china plate and Nate saw his mother trying to set the dish down with a shaky hand.

"Mother, are you well?" He was next to her in a heartbeat, taking the dish from her trembling fingers. "You look pale and your hands are ice cold."

"It's been an exciting day, that's all, and I need a rest. We can gather again for supper." She rose slowly and Hannah hurried to her side. "If you'll excuse me?"

Nathaniel decided he would send an invitation to Dr. Goodman that afternoon. His mother would be examined by the physician whether she liked it or not. In the meantime, he had guests to entertain.

"Lady Eliza, would you like a tour of Pendle Place?" he asked, holding out his arm. "I admit I'm quite proud of the manor and the estates."

"As he should be," added Grace. "At twelve, he learned how to manage the estate, eventually paid off his father's debts, and made wise investments."

"You make it sound much more astounding than it really was. I had the best advice and an excellent steward." Nate shook his head. "I managed not to repeat the mistakes of my father or make any major blunders."

"Modesty is another of his qualities," she said with a grin.

"Good God, soon there will be poems in my honor." Lady Eliza had taken his arm, and he took the lead out into the garden. "Do you read poetry, my lady?"

Her flaxen hair caught the sun as they descended the steps into the manicured, neatly plotted gardens. He was no Byron or Donne, but this woman made him feel romantic.

"Please, call me Eliza, and I do enjoy poetry," she answered. "I-I've even written some."

"There's an accomplishment. I can't imagine the mishmash I would make trying to put words of love on paper. It would be a waste of fine vellum...Eliza."

He watched her inhale deeply, taking in the scent of spring, and exhale. As she did so, her body relaxed. She reminded him of a wren with a broken wing he'd found as a child. His mother had told him to do away with it. Instead he had fixed a small cage for the bird and fed it some fruit. It had rewarded him with a song, its voice clear and loud for such a tiny creature. It was that hidden strength which convinced him not to give up on the bird. Yes, Eliza was his wren with a broken wing. With patience and care, she would sing again.

"There are only two kinds of men: the righteous who think they are sinners and the sinners who think they are righteous."

Blaise Pascal

Chapter Eight

London
The Following Week

The Marquess of Landonshire was pleased. Fate seemed to be smiling down at him for a change, and he whistled a cheery tune as he strolled along Pall Mall Street toward his destination. White and pink blossoms colored the bare tree limbs that lined the avenue. Lilacs had begun to bloom, and the sweet scent hung heavy in the air. He'd been to White's the night before and came away one hundred pounds plumper in the pocket. His card had been sent to the Falsbury townhouse, announcing his intention to make a morning call. Yes, he would collect Eliza and promptly take her over to Bellum's and seal the bargain.

His partner had the documents prepared and ready for signatures. It was as easy as selling a fine piece of horse flesh. Except his daughter would bring him much more. Thirty thousand pounds would pay off his debts, perhaps buy back a couple of the properties he'd been forced to sell, and set him up with a comfortable annual income. It had all worked out well enough. Why did the little doxy care about the man's age? Christ, Bellum wouldn't last more than five or ten years and she'd be free. A rich widow once again. She should be thanking him. Addle-pated women. They didn't understand business. His hounds had more sense than a female.

Landonshire stopped in front of the brick home, faced with expensive white-gray Portland stone. Sunny yellow daffodils and tulips in red and orange brightened the windowsills. His own rowhouse had been one of the first things to go when the first venture failed. No matter. His wife didn't accompany him to London since the Boldon shrew had died, and he preferred the hotel. Less expensive, good food and liquor, and close to his office and other...entertainment. He fingered the perfectly tied white cravat, double-checked the buttons on his new single-breasted dove gray tailcoat, and flicked a speck of dust from the white trousers. Removing his matching silk hat and smoothing back his hair, he opened the gate and ascended the stone steps.

The brass knocker held a miniature lion's head. Landonshire grasped it and rapped sharply three times. A butler promptly answered.

"May I help you?" he said in the stiff, indifferent tone of a well-trained servant.

"Lord Landonshire, Lady Eliza's father." He smiled benevolently at the man, pleased at the warm day, the sunshine, and his upcoming windfall. It had been an ugly few years, but it was all behind him now. "I believe I'm expected."

"Ah, indeed you are." The butler stepped to the side, opened the door wide, and waited patiently for coat and hat.

"No need, I shan't be here long."

The butler nodded. "Very well, sir. Follow me, please."

He took in the great expanse of the entry as he ambled over the marble floor. Halfway down the hallway, a door stood ajar. The servant stopped at the threshold.

"Lord Landonshire," he announced with a bow.

Entering the study, he was surprised to see both Lord and Lady Falsbury. The marquess sat behind a large oak desk with intricately carved square legs, his hands folded and resting on the glossy top, a stack of papers neatly piled next to him. Two leather chairs flanked the high desk, the lady seated on the right. He bowed to both host and hostess and took the vacant chair.

"Is Eliza on her way down?" he asked politely. "She's more like her mother every day. Always late, never a thought to time or appointments. It's a female trait, I suppose."

His chuckle faded from the glare cast by Lady Falsbury. "I *don't* suppose it is. Eliza has been with us for several years now, and she's proven to be very punctual."

"Beg your pardon, madam." He struggled for another thread of conversation. "I'm looking forward to seeing my granddaughter again. I imagine she's grown since the last time I held her." He turned his lips up in his most charming smile.

"I'm afraid not," said Falsbury without rising.

"She's a sickly thing, then? My daughter was puny as a child but look at her now."

"I'm afraid that won't be possible," Falsbury said as he sat back in the overstuffed leather chair, an odd look on his face.

His jaw ticked in irritation. "What won't be possible?" A finger of apprehension scratched at his gut.

Falsbury steepled his hands, a bland expression on his face. "I'm afraid you won't be meeting with your daughter."

"Is my sweet Eliza ill? My poor little girl. I'm in town for the week. I can come back in a day or two." This put a damper on his plans, but Bellum would have to understand. "Like I said, she's always had a delicate disposition."

"Really, Lord Landonshire? I think she's quite resilient surviving a childhood under your roof." The marchioness faced him, accusation in her dark brown eyes.

He blinked. Her tone hit him like a bunch of fives in the face. What had that little hoyden told them? His face burned hot; his heart pounded. He leaned forward, ignoring the addle-pate, and turned his attention to the marquess. Idiot women.

"Falsbury, what the devil is going on? Where the hell is my daughter?"

"On a ship to America."

"I want her down—what?" He ran a hand over his face. "This is not amusing."

Falsbury stood. "I agree. Nothing about you or your despicable tactics are amusing. But your game is up, and the bread and butter you were counting on is no longer on the table."

"I'm her father. She has no right taking my granddaughter and sailing off to—"

"You have *no* rights when it comes to Althea. Not a court in England would allow you custody." Lady Falsbury stood. "From what I understand, you couldn't afford a barrister without selling Eliza."

Landonshire's fingers curled into a fist, his jaw set. "I'm within my rights to punish my wife and child as I see fit. I've broken no laws." Oh how he wanted to slap the smug look off her face. "And how would you know about my finances? If that little maggot pie has been telling her lies again, she'll be sorry."

"I'm afraid you are the only sorry creature here, my lord." Falsbury's eyes burned a direct path to Landonshire's fist. "And if you raise those knuckles even a hairbreadth, I will enjoy beating you to a bloody pulp."

Panic skittered through his body like a rat in a dark alley. It ran down his spine, through his chest, and into his belly. What in blasted tarnation had just happened? Ten minutes ago, he'd been high on the ropes, and now his bright future was sliding into the gutter. He'd make the little whore pay when he got his hands on her.

"Explain this to me, real slow, since I'm obviously not comprehending." He sucked in a breath to calm his temper. Falsbury's older family name had more influence than his with or without the debts. But that didn't give him the right to interfere with Landonshire's property. And his most valuable asset was no longer within his grasp. "Eliza and the baby have left for America. Now how did she manage to make all those arrangements in a week's time without anyone knowing?"

"I made the arrangements after you threatened *my* granddaughter. Then I fired the new gardener. I do not take kindly to spies on my property. Eliza and Althea were on a ship at first light the day after your visit to the cemetery. It's an expensive journey, and I'm not inclined to tell you where in that vast country she might settle." Falsbury crossed his arms. "This interview has come to an end."

Something wasn't right here. He could smell it. "I think the whole story is a clanker. You wouldn't send them away just to spite me. I bet they're still at your country house."

"I would do anything, and I mean anything within in my power to keep my granddaughter safe. She is the child of my dead son and will never know the pain your daughter has."

Landonshire's lip curled. "I will track them down. I'm resourceful, you see, and persistent."

"Let me make this very clear, my lord." Falsbury straightened, his chest wide and body still lean and muscular. "No one endangers my family. Especially a coward who takes his own incompetence out on those weaker and dependent on him. I know your game. Eliza didn't need to say a word. My solicitor informed me that you sold her dowry property. I know she asked him to send bank notes in your name on several occasions. Unlike you, sir, I am a scrupulous businessman, and nothing goes on in my realm without my knowledge."

Sweat broke out on Landonshire's forehead. He resisted the urge to wipe it away. Damnation, he wouldn't give the pompous ass the satisfaction. "I made some bad investments during the war. I had to recoup my losses, and the property was mine to begin with."

"No, it belonged to your wife as part of *her* widow's dowry," countered Lady Falsbury.

Good God, he'd like to shut that woman up. If she were his wife...

"You pitched the gammon to my son after the wedding, trying to get him involved with one of your peep-o-day schemes. Another catastrophe. Every business venture you've attempted, except with Bellum, turned to dust. The only thing keeping you from debtor's prison is your title." Falsbury gave a tight smile. "Unfortunately, short of treason there isn't much I can do about that, or we wouldn't be having this conversation." Falsbury put both hands on the desk and leaned forward. "If I were you, I would take my losses and scuttle back to my estate like the weasel I am. Or *my* spies will see what they can dig up."

"I'll find her, by Christ. Mark my words. You'll pay for this."

Landonshire turned on his heel, leaving a string of foul words behind him. He stormed down the steps, his heels clicking on the pavement as he hailed a hackney. Bellum would be irate. Good, it would give him an ally in the next plot. Nobody crossed the Marquess of Landonshire, not without a reckoning.

The previous Lord Sunderland had crossed him. The whoremonger should have agreed to *any* business proposal by his own father-in-law straight away. Instead, he'd *checked into it*. The bloody ninny hadn't even had the decency to decline in person. Landonshire received a letter from his son-in-law's solicitor. Ah, but revenge had been sweet.

He grinned, a warmth spreading through his body as he remembered that night. The earl was known for being a rake and a drunkard. It had been easy enough to pay someone to challenge Sunderland. The fool never turned down a horse race. No one had questioned the fall or checked the tack for a cut in the girth. It had been Landonshire's good luck the horse had stumbled. But Sunderland had been an excellent rider. Without the tampered equipment, he would have stayed in the saddle sober or drunk.

Now the little widow was trying to thwart him. He imagined his hand around Eliza's pale slim neck, squeezing the life from her, face purple and eyes bulging. The image sent blood rushing to his groin. His manhood throbbed, anticipating the pain he would cause when he found her. If Bellum changed his tune, he would kill the ungrateful slut. The thought put a smile back on his face.

⌒

Bellum stared at him, disgust in his red-rimmed gray eyes. The office was dark, the sun outside barely penetrating the dusty windowpanes. He wiped a hand over his bald head then pulled at the fuzzy gray bits surrounding his ears.

"She's left the country? Did you send anyone out to check the docks? See when—or if—a vessel was bound for the colonies. A lovely woman and her young daughter would surely be noticed." Bellum squinted, raising his glasses from his nose to get a better look at Landonshire. "Wait, let me guess. You came straight here."

"Well, er, yes. I thought you might have an idea of what to do." Why did this ancient cur always make him feel dimwitted? If it wasn't for the money...

"I thought you might have an idea of what to do," Bellum mimicked. "Do you have a brain of your own? Blast it, man. Get your bollocks down to Bow

Street and hire a runner to find out what the hell is going on. That's my bride." The old man's silver brows pushed together. "Don't try to go yourself, or word will get out you're snooping around. If she hasn't left yet, and gets wind we're on to her, the chit will disappear again.

"My offer stands for one month. After that, I call in your vowels." Bellum licked his thin lips and smiled, a center gap exposing a pointy tongue, surrounded by pointy yellowish-brown teeth. His skin resembled a piece of gray parchment, crinkled up then smoothed back out. "My collectors can be very persuasive. I'll take your house, send you off to the widow's quarters, and keep the wife. You married her young—sixteen wasn't she? Even if your weak seed stopped filling her belly, she could still bear a babe of mine. I'm no member of the peer. Why should I care if my heir is a bastard? He'll still have blue blood."

Landonshire's mouth fell slack. Then the slow burn began, the fire that could only be put out by pain. Someone else's pain. "Careful, you old codger. Don't threaten a man who has nothing left to lose."

"There is in every true woman's heart, a spark of heavenly fire, which lies dormant in the broad daylight of prosperity, but which kindles up and beams and blazes in the dark hour of adversity."

Washington Irving

Chapter Nine

Pendle Place
Durham County

It had been a glorious week, but her dear friend would soon be leaving. They had all fallen into some type of routine. Eliza, Nathaniel, Grace, and Kit would ride out in the mornings before breakfast. Part of the property ran along the River Wear, and Lady Hannah had shown them the best spot for picnics. In the afternoons, there were also walks in the garden, croquet, or lawn bowls. Althea would accompany them, and Mrs. Watkins would spend an hour or two at the stables or enjoy some peaceful solitude.

There was afternoon tea in the drawing room or outside under the gazebo with Lady Pendleton, who had recuperated quickly but still was not quite herself, according to Hannah. Dr. Goodman, delayed by several emergencies, had arrived that morning. Lady Pendleton had assured him that she was fine, and he should concentrate on enjoying his visit. So in the evenings after supper, the group would play charades or cards. Hannah played the pianoforte beautifully with Grace or Nathaniel lending their steady voices. She had been surprised at Nathaniel's deep, clear tenor.

Eliza wished this time could go on forever. She'd never been so happy, felt so carefree. Althea thrived under the attentions of so many caring adults, and any shyness the toddler felt had disappeared by the second day. She had taken a particular liking to Nathaniel, perhaps due to his silly antics. He would get on his hands and knees and let her climb onto his back. Putting a hand behind his back to brace her, little hands clutching his collar and legs gripping his waist, he'd take her for a ride on a runaway horse. The game would end with a tickling match. Yesterday, they had engaged everyone in an ugly face contest, screwing up their features and demanding a vote on who looked the most hideous or terrifying. Ridiculous should have been a category.

Today Grace and Eliza sipped tea under the pavilion, breathing in the

scent of lilac and chatting about the previous day's picnic.

"What are you thinking about?" asked Grace, pushing a gold-red curl behind her ear. "Lord Pendleton?"

She blushed. "About the entire week. I wish you didn't have to leave."

"If the architect wasn't arriving from London, I would stay. But certain renovations need to be finished before winter. Though I must admit, there are days when I think getting that ancient fort into livable condition will be a life's achievement."

"I was looking forward to seeing it." Eliza bit her lip, hesitating to ask. "Are you trying yet for another baby?"

Sadness passed over Grace's face but disappeared with a smile. "We aren't *not* trying. The work on Sunderland keeps me busy and my mind off whether I'm with child."

Eliza reached over and squeezed her friend's hand. "You will have a beautiful baby, I know it. I feel it here," she said, her hand over her heart.

"Speaking of hearts," Grace began with an impish smile, "what do you think of Nate? He's quite taken with you."

"He's everything you've described over the years. And handsome. But don't start matchmaking. None of your plans for the two of us."

"Me?" Grace's eyes widened. "Except the two of you are a striking couple. It's obvious you're attracted to one another."

"It would never work."

"Why?" Grace picked up a biscuit and nibbled at it. "He has a title, money, looks. He's kind and intelligent with a sense of humor. Pendleton is quite a catch."

"He could do so much better than a widow already with a child. Especially a widow such as myself." She hated the self-pity in her voice, but it was true. "He should have someone...better."

Grace gave an indelicate snort. "That's absurd. I wish I could go to one of London's fine shops and buy you some confidence. Or a magical mirror so you could see yourself as others do."

"And that's why I love you, Gracie."

"We have the same strength, cousin. Only mine shows on the outside, and yours hides on the inside. You see yourself as weak because of your past. Yet, I see you as resilient and a survivor. I don't know if I could have survived your childhood."

"I would need that magic mirror to view myself in that light," Eliza murmured.

"You're quite a catch yourself. Young, beautiful, a nice widow's jointure and some property to bring along to the next marriage. And Althea is proof you can *breed,* as the men put it when they think we aren't listening." She popped the last bite into her mouth and took a sip of tea to wash it down. "Seriously, are you happy here? Will these arrangements be suitable for a few weeks?"

"I am quite satisfied. More so than I imagined. The Pendletons are an excellent family and I'm growing quite fond of Hannah. I'm more concerned Thea won't want to leave."

Eliza sighed, wondering about this newfound contentment, so unfamiliar yet welcome. She watched Althea play with her doll under a tree, while Mrs. Watkins lay sprawled out on a blanket spread over the tender spring grass.

"What on-dits are we discussing, ladies?" asked Hannah as she took a chair and poured a cup. Adding a lump of sugar, she sipped it, grinned, and added another. "Mother says I will be broad as a sow if I don't mind my sugar."

Grace giggled. "You do snort rather well, but I hardly think you'll grow fat."

"Anyone for a game of Spillikins?" She set the box on the table.

"What will we play for?" asked Eliza. She knew Grace's competitive nature always liked a prize. "A shilling?"

"You've only been here a week, and already we have you gambling!" Hannah laughed. "How about a ribbon? We each choose one of our best, and the winner gets her pick."

"Perfect. A ribbon it is." Grace opened the box and dumped out the thin ivory sticks.

They took turns removing a stick from the jumble until one of the other pieces shifted. Eliza used one of the blunted sticks in her own growing pile to remove an especially tricky one on top.

"That lacy lavender ribbon will go well with my eyes, don't you think?" She laughed at Grace's frown. "My how you hate to lose!"

"It's not the losing, it's being bested."

Hannah rolled her eyes. "You're splitting hairs, as always. By the way, is Althea taking a nap?"

Eliza shook her head. "No, she's..." Mrs. Watkins lay still on the blanket, a doll next to her, and no Althea. Dread gripped her throat. "Oh, God."

The women jumped from their chairs, the table wobbling precariously as the ivory sticks clattered to the ground.

"Mrs. Watkins! Wake up, Althea is gone." Eliza gulped air, trying to push back the panic. She ran into the small wooded area, calling her daughter's name. Decaying leaves and wet soil assaulted her nostrils. The sun left a speckled pattern through the leaves of the tall oaks but the grove was empty. "ALTHEA!"

"I'm sure she didn't wander far. Let's split up." Grace took charge, calm as always, pointing each of them in a different direction. "Mrs. Watkins, please go to the house and tell Nate."

"Tell me what?" he asked, coming from the stables, crop in hand.

"Althea is missing. She hasn't been gone long but..."

Eliza knew the second Grace's thoughts ran with hers. She looked at Nathaniel, his face grim.

"I'll get Cyrano. Find me something that has her scent on it." He ran back to the stables and the kennels.

"Cyrano?" Eliza did not have time to wait on anything or anyone. Her arms trembled, the deep breaths not enough to keep the anxiety at bay.

"Nate's best blood hound. He can pick up a scent and follow it till doomsday." Hannah grabbed the doll. "This will work. Bring it to my brother."

Hannah picked up her skirts and hurried in the direction Grace had pointed. As Eliza ran after Nathaniel, she could hear the women calling over and over for Althea. *Oh God, please don't let him have her. Please.*

Cyrano was a large black and tan hound with droopy eyes and long ears. His head reached Pendleton's thigh as he held the doll under the dog's nose. They jogged back to the blanket and had the animal sniff again. His ears dragged across the grass and dirt as his nose went to work. He entered into the woods and out again, back in to wind around several trees and out once more. The same pattern one would expect of a toddler ambling along.

Then his nose pointed toward the sky, and he grew still. A long, mournful bay sounded, and the dog's nose went back to the ground, and he picked up his pace. Nathaniel grabbed her hand, and they trotted after him. The other women's voices grew faint.

Eliza's stomach twisted into a knot. "What if my father has taken her?"

"He hasn't."

"How do you know?" She desperately wanted to believe him.

"Cyrano is moving too quickly. She's close."

Hope surged in her chest. The tears blurred her vision, and she gripped Nathaniel's hand tighter, stumbling after him.

They came to a meadow on the other side of the woods. A large rowan tree stood in the center. A flash of yellow interrupted the shade of the low branches. A small yellow frock. "Althea!"

Cyrano began his long, mournful howl again and trotted toward the scent. Eliza ran after the animal. "Don't hurt her."

Nathaniel laughed behind her. The dog reached the sleeping child, sniffed her thoroughly, and let out another long yowl. Tail wagging, he slurped his long tongue across the little girl's face. Fully awake now, she squealed in delight and threw her arms around the canine's neck. "Puppy!"

Eliza sank onto the grass and pulled Althea to her, swiping at her own wet cheeks. "Oh, my baby. Oh my sweet, naughty baby." She rocked the wiggling girl back and forth, Cyrano still trying to lick her face and getting Eliza's cheek in the process.

Laughter bubbled up her throat. This sad-eyed, slobbering dog had found her little girl. "Cyrano, you are my hero."

"Wait a minute," objected Nathaniel. "I set him on the trail."

Althea grabbed the dog's wet jowls with her hands and kissed his nose. "Hewo, my hewo."

"Pfft! The fickle female lives on." Nathaniel picked up Althea and hauled her onto his shoulders. "Enough excitement for one day, little one. I don't think your mama can take much more."

He held out his hand to Eliza and she took it, the touch chasing away the panic and warming her cold fingers. As her racing heart slowed, she studied Nate's profile. He still held her hand, while the other grasped a small foot that had left grass stains on his pristine white shirt. Her eyes strayed to the form-fitting buckskin breeches and shiny black boots then back to their clasped hands. Nathaniel sang a little ditty to Althea, who tried to sing along, her hands clasped under his chin. As the song's momentum picked up, her chubby legs beat against his barrel chest as he sang, and his grip tightened, his shoulders stretching the fine material of his blue riding coat. Her heart eased, her muscles relaxed, and she began to enjoy the walk. Her daughter looked as if she belonged climbing on this man's back, kissing his cheek or his shoulders. Everything about this scene seemed...natural.

"Mama, sing. Sing wif us."

These two had become fast friends over the week, and Althea looked for Nathaniel after breakfast each morning. As all three picked up the tune again, Cyrano added his low yelp to the voices, sending everyone into a fit of the giggles. Eliza suddenly wondered what it would be like to have a family, an entire family. She wanted more children some day.

"Oh, my lady, I'm so sorry. I'm so sorry," cried Mrs. Watkins, running up to them as they emerged onto the lawn. Her voice was hoarse, her eyes puffy. "I've been praying and calling."

"We found her in the meadow, or I should say Cyrano found her." Nathaniel reassured the distraught woman.

"I'm just thankful the darling is safe. I'd never have a decent night's sleep again if anything had happened to that baby." The governess dabbed at her eyes with a handkerchief and blew her nose. "I'll go pack now, I just had to know she was safe before I left. I'm ever so sorry, ever so sorry."

"Mrs. Watkins, wait." Eliza's voice cracked. "You forgot someone."

The portly woman turned. "I understand if you've lost trust in me, my lady. If I hadn't fallen asleep—"

"None of us saw her wander off. She's *my* daughter and my ultimate responsibility. I have every faith you will be *more* than zealous watching over her after this. I know I will. It can happen so quickly."

"Your ladyship is more than generous. I said you were a gift from heaven when you first hired me." She made the sign of the cross and wiped her eyes again.

"Now, please take Althea, change her clothes, and clean her up. She has dog...kisses all over her." Eliza wrinkled her nose. "I thought my daughter gave the sloppiest kisses, but she's met her match with Cyrano."

"Yes, ma'am. Of course," cried Mrs. Watkins, tears still trickling down her cheeks as she reached for the toddler. "Come along, child. Give me a hug!"

The pair went into the house, and Eliza felt like one of those air balloons she'd read about, once the flame had been extinguished. Utterly and completely drained.

"Are you all right?" he asked.

She nodded, tears collecting again. This time tears of relief. "I was so frightened. If anything happened to her, I don't know..." It came full force then, that kind of sobbing that has been pushed back for so long, it will no longer be contained.

Nathaniel's arms came around her, pulled her close, and she buried her face in his hard chest. Her body shook with a tidal wave of emotion that demanded release. Fear, anger, even the hatred toward her father. The strong, comforting arms around her offered the kind of solace she had always longed for, and she drew strength from his closeness. Eliza let the sorrow and self-pity float away on the salty waves running down her face and neck and clung to this man who was becoming such a precious part of her life in so short a time.

Nate gathered her close and rocked her back and forth, stroking her shoulders and hair. He murmured soft words in her ear, telling her all would be well, that she was safe with him. Her tears soaked his shirt, and still she cried. He remembered when he'd held Grace like this after her mother had died. She'd needed to purge herself of all the emotions that had cluttered her mind and burdened her soul. Eliza needed the same, and he'd give her as long as she needed. This moment had been building for a long time, years maybe.

Her fingers clutched at his lapels, but the weeping lessened. Her pulse slowed and she hiccupped. Nate looked into her eyes, darkened to indigo with her tears, and had never seen anything more lovely. He wanted to be her hero, her knight in shining armor. Scoop her up in his arms and kiss away her tears. She hiccupped again.

"I must look a fright," she said, a watery smile curving her full lips.

He cursed his riding coat for not having a pocket. "I'm sorry I don't have a handkerchief." He moved his hands to her face and wiped her cheeks with his thumbs, then without thought, ran the pad over her full mouth.

Her eyes widened and he saw the need—and uncertainty—in those violet orbs. Her lips parted and he did what seemed natural. Nate pressed his mouth to hers, the barest brush of his lips. The action heated his blood, pulse racing as he pulled back slowly, and searched her face for a sign of regret. Instead, with tremulous fingers, she reached up and drew his head down, offering another kiss. His hands pushed through her thick mane, silky and sensual against his skin. Her body fit against him like a second half, as if she were something he'd been searching for all his life. The missing piece to the puzzle.

"Did you find—" Grace's voice broke the spell.

Eliza jerked from his grasp, the low-cut blue and violet flowered dress revealed creamy breasts rising and falling as she panted. Her warmth slipped away from him, and he felt its loss.

"Oh, my. I assumed Cyrano found Althea from the howls, but it seems my brother was just as successful as the hound," Hannah said to Grace.

"I was only... then Eliza began to cry... If you breathe a word of this, I'll hang you both by your thumbs and—"

Laughter drowned out the rest of his threat. To his relief, Eliza smiled shyly, picked up her skirts, and ran to the house. His two female nemeses flanked him.

"Where did you find Althea?"

"Is she all right?"

"Where is Mrs. Watkins? Poor thing was in bad loaf, wailing and sniffling."

Nate sighed. "Althea was in the meadow under the rowan, Cyrano is hero for the day, and Mrs. Watkins is appropriately contrite and extremely relieved."

"And Eliza?" asked Grace, a mischievous gleam in her green eyes.

He grinned. A big stupid grin that he couldn't wipe off his face. *Good God, this is what Kit warned me about.*

"I saw the Cloud, though I did not foresee the Storm."

Daniel Defoe

Chapter Ten

Early May

Eliza saw the familiar Falsbury seal on the envelope and clutched it to her chest. She wished Grace was still here to read this with her. Her cousin was a pillar of strength.

Please be good news.

Not that she was in a hurry to leave. She loved this beautiful estate and was growing close to Hannah and Lady Pendleton. And then there was Nathaniel. Nate, he had asked her to call him last night as they walked in the garden with Lady Hannah. They had not been alone again since Althea had wandered off and...the kiss, which had caused both disappointment and relief. It would not have been proper, even as a widow.

The attraction between them had grown. A look across the table, his hand a moment too long on the small of her back, a shared smile. Her heat fluttered each time he walked into the room. Her nights were filled with his kiss, reliving it in her dreams over and over, each time adding a touch or caress. She would wake with a throbbing low in her belly, her body covered in sweat from a desire she'd never felt before, even with Carson.

With a deep breath, she sat at her toilette and opened the letter.

Dearest Eliza,

I hope this finds you well and my granddaughter happy. We miss you both dreadfully and hope to see you soon. Grace wrote to explain the circumstances of your new residence. I knew Lady Pendleton years ago when we were both girls, and she is a gracious woman. I trust your stay there will be pleasant.

We went to London and met with Landonshire. I wish you could have seen the look on his face when he found out you were not there. Falsbury was brilliant, calling his bluff and almost sending your father into an apoplectic fit. Chester hasn't enjoyed himself so much in years. It almost came to fisticuffs, but Landonshire is a coward at heart. He left pell-mell, most likely to confer with the despicable Mr. Bellum.

Though you are presently safe, Falsbury does not think the matter is closed. Your father will check the ships that have left dock and send out more spies, no doubt. I'm afraid there may be only one way to keep you permanently out of his reach. We must find you a suitable husband. This is not a conclusion we came to easily since I would be devastated if you left us. But my husband pointed out my selfishness in this matter, and our honor demands we present this option to you in the best light.

If you are married to another, Landonshire will give up his foolish scheme. You cannot hide at Pendle Place forever. Both you and Althea deserve to be happy and loved. Please consider your future choices carefully until we see you again.

L. Falsbury

Marriage? Eliza stood and paced the length of the room. *Pish and perdition!* Marriage to a suitable husband. *One closer to my age.* It made sense but to open herself up again to another man... She was damaged property, certainly no great match for anyone despite her bloodline. Especially once her father's financial situation became common London on-dit. Where would she find someone? It wasn't as if she could traipse off to London for a season. She'd be discovered as soon as she re-entered society.

Tears pricked the back of her lids, and she closed her eyes. It would not help to cry. As much as she loved it here, Eliza knew the marchioness was right. *Breathe in...and out. In...and out.* Althea needed a father who would dote on her like Nate. *Nate!* If only he weren't such a good man, perhaps they might have made a match. No, he deserved so much more than a flawed, fearful wife. He should have a confident, intelligent, beautiful woman who would never cringe from an unexpected shout or startle at a sudden wave of a stranger's hand. Besides, Hannah had said he planned to look for a wife when she attended her first season next year. Nate could have his pick of women in London. He didn't need to settle for a widow and another man's child.

Scotland. Yes, her mother had family in Scotland. She could take Althea across the border and hide with relatives. Landonshire hated the Scots, so it would be highly unlikely he would search for her there. Nor would he ever believe she had enough backbone to search out strangers. Yet, there might be a life there, a kind Highlander who would not mind raising a little girl if she could give him sons in return. She had a property through Carson. Falsbury and Sunderland would help her arrange for the sale to provide a dowry. And of course her income would be maintained until she remarried. *If* she remarried. She had a vision of a lovely cottage, tucked in the hills, with a clear stream running behind it.

Eliza pressed her head to the cool glass of the window. As Nate would say, she'd read too many romantic novels.

Ezra Maxwell slammed the ledger closed with a smile. "April proved to be a good month, my lord. Our losses were minimal for the lambing season, and the hay is coming up nicely. If we don't get too much rain, we might even get three cuttings out of it this year."

"Excellent. Then I can turn my mind to other matters."

"I know something is on your mind. It wouldn't be a certain female, would it?" His steward grinned broadly. "Lady Eliza is a fine bit of muslin."

"Yes, well. I'm more concerned about her future. It's been three weeks and Landonshire has had enough time to figure out she's not on a ship." Nate ran a hand through his hair. "I wish there was a way

to keep her safe permanently. It would ease my mind."

"There is, of course."

"Short of posting armed sentries, I don't know what." He rubbed the back of his neck, irritated at his helplessness. "I swear, I'd do anything to keep Eliza and that little girl safe."

"Marry her," said Maxwell quietly.

"Marry her?" He hadn't meant for his voice to sound so incredulous.

"She's a widow and doesn't need her father's permission. Falsbury is in charge of her jointure. There'd be no reason for her father to harass the girl if she were someone else's wife. His plan would be null and void." The steward paused as the idea took root in Nate's head. "Unless of course, you aren't fond of her?"

"Of course I'm fond of her."

"Perhaps the idea of taking on another man's child bothers you." The steward placed the ledger back on the shelf.

"No! I adore Althea."

"Then if it were me, I'd leg-shackle myself to the girl and save myself the torture of looking for a wife in London next year. I've heard you talk about those *soirées*. Rather have a tooth pulled, I think."

Nate stared at his steward, his mouth slack.

"Don't look so shocked at the suggestion. I've seen the two of you together." He picked up his hat and fitted it to his head. "But that's just what I'd do." He walked out of the study whistling a bawdy tavern tune.

Hannah was playing the pianoforte when he entered the parlor. Eliza looked up from a book and smiled. He had grown accustomed to seeing her each evening. After Grace and Kit left, Nate had returned to the duties of the estate and only saw his guests in the morning and evening. How he looked forward to the evenings.

Eliza had read extensively and, once comfortable with him, sparred well in debates on politics and philosophy. They had not been without a chaperone since the day he kissed her. The mere thought of her touch sent him in search of the cold waters of the River Wear. It was more than physical though. They had much in common besides Grace. Both enjoyed horseback riding and chess, and they shared the same philosophies in life. He appreciated the way she would listen quietly, and then think about her answer before giving an opinion. She treated Mrs. Watkins with respect and did not look down on others because of their birth. When he'd commented on this, Eliza responded that those who were born to privilege had an obligation to those who were not. It had sounded like something Maxwell would say.

Now that his estate manager had made his approval of Lady Eliza known, she'd been on his mind even more than before. When Maxwell had planned a tour of the properties to introduce her in the village, Nate explained the need for secrecy. The man never blinked. The next day he'd invited her instead to witness the end of their lambing season. Neither man had been able to decide which event was more delightful to watch—the birth of the lamb, Eliza's observation, or Althea playing with the wobbly newborns.

And then there was Althea. Nate had grown fond of the little chit. No, if he were honest, he was quite smitten. Trying to figure out some of her speech had turned into an amusing game for he and Hannah. She'd enchanted the entire household. The head groom had a pony saddled for her daily. Cyrano had become her constant companion. The hound followed her everywhere, even slept next to her bed. It had put Eliza's mind at ease to know the dog watched over her. His howl would wake the dead if anyone approached the child.

"Hmm, your brother looks far away tonight."

He blinked at the sound of her deep husky voice. "Good evening, my lovely ladies," he said with a bow. "I'm distracted by such beauty."

"Gah!" cried Hannah, rolling her eyes and not missing a note on the keys.

He took a seat next to Eliza and peeked at the title of the book she held.

"*Waverly*. The historical novel with romance, by the not-so-anonymous author Walter Scott. Do you like it?"

"I do. Have you read it?"

"No, the Scottish Uprising, death, and multiple lost loves don't appeal to me for leisurely reading. I prefer something thoughtful like Thomas Paine."

Eliza closed the book. "Do you believe the unknown author of the series is Walter Scott?"

"The *ton* certainly thinks so. I've only read his poetry so I wouldn't try to presume. I do think he's a bit of a coward not to put his name on it." He leaned back against the loveseat, their bodies almost touching. If he took a very deep breath, their shoulders would touch. "It's warm in here. Care for a stroll in the garden?"

"Oh, yes. Hannah, a walk?"

His sister looked up from the pianoforte. "Go ahead, I'll be right behind you. I need to...get this chord figured out first."

Nate stood and held out his hand. She took it, pink spreading across her cheeks as he pulled her toward him. Dropping her fingers, he held out his arm. "We'll stay close until you finish," he told Hannah as they walked by.

"No need, I can find you easily enough." She plunked at a combination of keys, concentration drawing her brows together.

They walked into the cool night air. The full moon above lit their path and bathed the plants and flowers with a golden glaze. He heard Eliza sigh, a soft contented sound that made his heart glad.

"Are you enjoying your stay here?"

She nodded. "I cannot express how happy Althea and I have been. I worry about Lady Pendleton though. I read to her for a bit this afternoon, but I could tell she was weak and her spirits low."

He nodded. "Dr. Goodman will see her again tomorrow before he leaves and make a diagnosis."

They walked around a circle of azaleas ready to bloom and continued down another walk. The full moon revealed her silhouette through the pale blue muslin, her golden tresses glowing in the evening light. Wisteria had bloomed along the trellis, the sweet scent still clinging to the white and red petals.

"You seemed distracted when you came into the parlor. Are you concerned for your mother?" she asked, her eyes sparkling even in the shadows.

"I'll be happy when we know what ails her. But Dr. Goodman will have her up and around in no time. I have complete faith in him."

"Yes, he seems like a fine doctor."

He was finally alone with Eliza, had a moment to say whatever he wanted, and they were making polite conversation. His chance would soon be gone.

"The truth is, you were on my mind, and our trip to the lambing shed. I enjoyed watching you and Althea." *I want to watch you every day.*

"We both enjoyed it immensely. Mr. Maxwell is a kind man to put up with us."

"Your daughter has commandeered my best hound too. She can't have him, you know." His laugh died away when a spasm of pain crossed her face. "Did I say something?"

She shook her head and turned away from him. An owl hooted in the distance. A flash of his yellow eyes gave away the bird's hiding place.

"Do you see him?" he asked in a low voice.

"The owl? No."

"It's there."

She tipped her head, searching in the direction he pointed.

"Here, follow my finger." He bent so that his head was just over her shoulder and they could follow the same path of vision. Then he straightened his arm until the tip of his finger lined up with the bird. "See it?"

She nodded. "He's beautiful."

"As are you," he whispered in her ear, his lips brushing her slender pale neck. Eliza stiffened beneath her touch.

"I apologize for taking liberties, but it could take another week to see you alone." He stilled, waiting to see if she would push away. Emboldened, he laid his cheek against her hair and breathed in the intoxicating smell of jasmine and mint. He closed his eyes, slowly put his arms around her, and moved against her back. Again, he stilled.

When her body relaxed and leaned back into his, he wanted to spin her in his arms, claim her mouth, ravish her with his tongue. She sighed, her head tipping back against his shoulder, her bodice tightening with the movement. His eyes traced the line of breasts, white against the moonlight, the curve of her jaw, the outline of a smile on her lips. She was exquisite. No other woman molded to him so perfectly, stirred his blood so quickly, or made him feel the need to protect so fiercely.

Maxwell's words came back to him. *Marry her*.

Marriage had always been a distant obligation he would someday fulfill. He had neither disliked nor been overly fond of the institution. His steward was happily married, but his parents union had been a disaster. The odds were evenly split whether he would find happiness.

Yet, with Eliza in his arms, he wondered how he would be happy without her.

"I've been thinking about your predicament," he began.

"As have I. Lady Falsbury wrote with a solution that I've been mulling over." Her voice sounded hesitant. "She feels that if I</I> were to choose a husband for myself, my father would be forced to find another avenue of finance."

"Yes, my steward and I had come to the same conclusion." Here was his chance if he wanted it. The opening Maxwell would see as a sign from the good Lord, himself.

Eliza pulled his hands down gently and turned. Tears gathered in her eyes as she stared at the buttons on his waistcoat. "Nate, I—"

He held her face in his hands, waited for her to look at him. The desire shone in her eyes. He touched his lips to hers, brushing one way then the other. Her gasp was hot against his mouth, and he dipped his head for a kiss. Her arms wrapped around his neck, pulling him down, and her lips parted for him.

Delving in, the sweetness of honey coated his tongue. Her taste, her smell, her touch was an aphrodisiac. His pulse pounded in his neck and sent jolts down his body. His desire became evident as a moan escaped his throat. She was everything he'd imagined love could be.

Love.

A cold shower couldn't have shocked him more as that word penetrated his brain. Her breathing was quick, her gaze searching his face, tears of disappointment swimming in her eyes. He tried to pull her close again and reassure her, but she took a step back.

"I-I..." Her hands clasped her stomach as if to settle it, pulling in deep breaths. "I have decided to take Lady Falsbury's advice. I shall write to Grace for an introduction to my mother's family in Scotland. Though I have never met them, I believe they would welcome Althea and me."

"Scotland? There's no need for you to leave." He reached for her again, but she took another step. "Eliza, I want you to stay."

She shook her head. "No, I cannot impose upon your hospitality indefinitely. I must think of my daughter and begin a new life. Here, we are in limbo. We cannot go back, and we cannot move forward."

Nate's chest tightened. It had never occurred to him she would leave, make other plans without conferring with him or Sunderland. He understood her reasons but selfishly wanted more time. More time to come to know her. More time to see if they were truly compatible. More time to see...if this was love.

"I will try to convince you otherwise, you know."

She nodded and closed the distance between them. Placing a hand on his cheek, she whispered, "You are such a good man. I wish I was worthy."

"There you two are," cried Hannah. "Those chords were harder to determine than I had anticipated."

His sister's guise did not fool him. She had purposely given them time alone and he was grateful. The interlude had only confirmed his attraction to this delectable widow. But did he want to marry her and spend the rest of his life with her? He had long ago sworn not to follow in his father's footsteps. When he took a wife, he would be faithful.

The conversation from earlier this afternoon echoed again in his head.

I'd leg-shackle myself to that girl up and save myself the torture of looking for a wife in London next year.

Lady Eliza was not an object to be bought or sold. She was pure of heart, intelligent and desirable. He would not marry her out of convenience.

As the trio returned to the house, his mind whirled with calculations. A message sent to Sunderland Castle and then a letter to Scotland and back would take time. He had several weeks to come to terms with his feelings and then persuade Eliza if he so desired.

And he had yet to coax the avenging angel out into the open again. Yes, there was still work to do before anyone left Pendle Place.

"And all who told it added something new, and all who heard it, made enlargements too."

Alexander Pope

Chapter Eleven

"What are you saying, Dr. Goodman?" Nate ran a hand over his face. "She's tired, weak, and distracted. I realize these are vague symptoms, but you can't give some kind of diagnosis?"

"You misunderstand. I said Lady Pendleton doesn't have a *physical* ailment."

"Then what the hell is wrong with her?"

He was frustrated. Women were so blasted exasperating. Nothing about them seemed simple. His mother was constantly fatigued yet not ill. Eliza was attracted to him but ready to bolt. Hannah grinned like a Cheshire cat at both of them yet said nothing to help. If he had a choice, he'd hide away with Maxwell, Thea, and Cyrano for a month to regain his sanity.

"Your mother is depressed. Specifically, she is feeling the pangs of guilt from years past." The physician accepted the glass of brandy the viscount offered. "I think the discussion of Hannah going to London next year has brought back memories."

"What in God's name does my mother have to feel guilty about?" His father had been the villain in their marriage. She'd been the caring parent, always present. It made no sense. The hideaway was sounding better.

"That is a conversation you need to have with Lady Pendleton." Dr. Goodman swirled the amber liquid, studying it for a moment before he took a sip. "I will say, if she can ease her conscience, her health will return."

"Has there been one simple female in the history of mankind?" Nate asked then threw back the last of his brandy. He let out a long breath and took the stopper out of the crystal decanter for another taste. "By Christ, this is not what I expected, though I'm glad it's not a serious illness."

"I wish I could have been more helpful. Tomorrow I'll stop by the village on my way home. Mrs. Stanley can bring up some valerian root to help her sleep. Lack of rest intensifies an emotional state. I've told Hannah to ensure she has a cup of chamomile tea after supper as well. The rest is up to her."

Mrs. Maxwell ladled stewed apples onto Nathaniel's plate, the tart fruit mixed with cinnamon and honey made his mouth water. She pinched his cheek and blew at the strands of red hair falling into her eyes as she added more slices to her husband's plate. The woman still made him feel like a boy of twelve. Ezra scooped another spoonful into his mouth.

"Eat, now. I cooked this up special for you."

"I've heard that about every meal I've eaten here." He winked at her and grinned at his steward. "I swear I'll steal her away some day."

"Those are fightin' words, my lord."

Nate sat back in his chair after the second helping and stretched out his legs. The cottage was well-kept and clean. They were in the kitchen, the room he had frequented since old enough to ride behind his father. Pots hung from hooks next to the fireplace. Stalks of coriander and basil, strung from the ceiling to dry, filled the air with a spicy pungent scent. Handwoven multicolored rugs kept the chill away and added to the room's coziness.

"I need some female advice."

"Haven't asked the girl to marry you yet?"

Nate chuckled. "No, and it's not that female. It's my mother."

His steward grunted and took another bite of the fruit. "Came to the wrong place for that. We ain't never seen eye to eye."

"Exactly. According to Dr. Goodman, my mother's malady isn't physical but mental. He believes it to be a case of conscience."

"Your father came back to haunt her." Maxwell let his spoon clatter onto the plate and patted his stomach. "You've done it again, love. I swear you're a gift from heaven above."

His wife giggled like a schoolgirl.

"I was hoping you could give me a clue to the cause of her guilt. I don't want to be hit on my blind side." He pushed his fingers through his hair. "Last night I dreamed I was a bastard. The result of my mother's flirtations with a groom. If you know of any dark family secrets, please bring them to light."

Maxwell chortled. "You are most definitely your father's son. There's more of him in you than you care to admit. We've had more than one argument on that point. I think your mother is an unhappy woman with many regrets over the years."

With a nod, Nate rose and took his riding coat from the back of a chair. "It was worth the trip just for the apples."

"About the other one. Don't wait too long. Indecision is the root of regret."

He paused, knowing his steward was referring to Eliza. The man knew him too well. "I just need to be sure."

"Of her feelings or yours?"

"It's not a matter of feelings. It's a matter of fidelity. I need to be sure I won't make the mistakes of my father. She deserves better than that." He locked eyes with Maxwell. "You say I'm my father's son, *and* he loved my mother. Yet he was unfaithful to her time and time again. What if I do the same to Eliza?"

"Does the girl love you?"

"It's not that simple."

"It is." The older man took out his pipe and tapped it against the table. "The key is reciprocity. She has to love you back."

Nathaniel found his mother in the library, a book in her lap, eyes closed. He sank into the leather wingback chair next to her, studying the Turkish rug of golds, blues, and reds. With the heel of his riding boot, he traced the swirling pattern.

"You should change for supper." Lady Pendleton smiled at her son. "Althea was looking for you earlier. She's as devoted to you as she is to that dog."

"I can't believe you allow Cyrano in the house."

"I'm getting mellow in my old age."

He snorted. "So it seems." He straightened and leaned his elbows on his knees. "And reminiscent?"

She pressed her lips together. "Yes, I suppose we should talk. Why don't you pour us both some claret?"

He rose and went to the side table, pouring wine for them both. Outside on the lawn, Althea kicked a ball at Cyrano. The hound howled and pushed it back with his nose, his ears trailing the ground. The little girl squealed, ran after it, and tripped. The dog was next to her as she fell on the grass, sniffing at her face and dragging his tongue across her cheek and neck. She grabbed his slobbery muzzle and kissed his nose. Nate's chest contracted.

Indecision is the root of regret.

"Is this about Hannah's season in London?" he asked.

"Indirectly."

He handed her a glass and sat down.

"I haven't been completely honest about your father and me...and our marriage." She swished the dark red liquid against the cut crystal, lost in thought again.

"I'm listening."

"When I met your father, he was the most handsome bachelor of the season, and had recently inherited the viscountcy. I was smitten—my head turned by all the girls who vied for his attention—yet he wanted *me*. I was never a beautiful woman, pretty and stately as my father used to say, but not beautiful.

"My mother pursued the match because the Pendletons were an old family and extremely wealthy. Since I was the daughter of an earl, his parents approved the union. We were married before the year was up."

Lady Pendleton paused, her eyes faraway. "We were so happy at first. Your father was charming, witty—he made me laugh. But as the months passed, his flaws became apparent. His lack of business sense, his overgenerous nature, his excessive spending were all weaknesses I despised. I harangued him at every turn, belittled each of his unsuccessful decisions. I wanted Pendleton to be strong like my father, so I tried to change him."

"I assume that didn't work." Nate studied his mother with narrowed eyes. She'd never admitted any wrongdoing when it came to the late viscount. A knot formed in his stomach. He had just walked onto a cliff with precarious footing.

"The passion still smoldered. As I said, he was a very attractive man, and I was young. It seemed the only thing he could do right in my eyes was…the physical side of our marriage. When you were born, things were better for a time. He was so proud of you, to have a son. Mr. Maxwell became the estate manager, and the property thrived until we had two seasons of rain."

Nate nodded. "Yes, that was the beginning of the estate's decline. Father made several bad ventures. Maxwell tried to warn him against the investments, but Father trusted the men and insisted the expenditures would replenish the accounts."

"Yes, and it wasn't only that. With the bad weather came the loss of crops, which affected the livestock. The villagers were struggling to survive. I felt bad for them, I did. But our own financial state was not good after the investments went sour. I'm ashamed to say..."

Damnation! What did she do?

"I told him if he gave another penny to those families, when our own future was so perilous, he would not be welcome back in my bed." She took a drink of the wine and leaned her head back against the chair. The lines around her light brown eyes and mouth seemed deeper. More gray streaked her ash-blonde hair than a month ago. "I began the criticism again, berating him for every decision. Now that I look back on it, I'm afraid he was damned no matter what he did."

"You were afraid, Mother. Fear can make us say things we don't mean."

"No, it was spite. He was lacking, in my eyes, and I resented him for it. My expectations have always been high, even with my children, I'm afraid. But your father was a gentle soul, and I wore him down until he believed what I believed."

"And what was that?"

"He was a failure, good for nothing but frivolity, and would never be the man I expected." A tear ran down her cheek. "I *did* love him but I didn't respect him, couldn't comprehend why he could not change, so my affection turned sour. I didn't try to understand the kind of man he was or *help* him become the kind of man I needed. In the end, I made us both miserable and pushed him into the arms of another woman. In a way, I am responsible for his death."

Nate ran a hand over his face. "Why are you telling me this now?"

"So you don't make the same mistake I did." Lady Pendleton leaned forward and took his hand. "With Eliza."

He was stunned. "All these years, you let me think there was not an ounce of good in my father. And now you tell me it was all a lie?"

She shook her head. "My mind needed to justify his death. I was as irresponsible as he had been by not taking any of the blame for our failed marriage. He never stopped trying until I pushed him away."

"What in God's name does this have to do with Eliza?" Bile rose in his throat along with the horrid thoughts he'd had about his father over the years. The disdainful comments that had always angered Maxwell.

"She has that same generosity of spirit, that innate kindness your father had. I considered him pathetic by the time your sister was born. As I grew older and wiser, I realized I'd misinterpreted goodness for weakness. I disregarded his loyalty and threw it in his face, for it had no value to me." His mother's voice cracked. "Strength can be hidden deep inside a person. He never gave up on me, on our marriage, until the very end.

"When I found out the London on-dits portrayed me as a shrew and he the victim, I flew into a rage and said such hateful things. I told him I didn't care if he lived or died, I only wanted him out of my sight. That was the night he found comfort with another man's wife. The woman had a terrible reputation, and your father was an easy mark. To save face, I insinuated that he'd had many other affairs."

"You lied?"

She covered her face with her hands and nodded. "It was the only time he was unfaithful to me."

He couldn't breathe for a moment; her words punched him in the gut. His jaw clenched as the information sank in. "All this time you have let me hate my father? By Christ, if you were not my mother, I'd call you out."

He stood and walked back to the window, watching Althea and the dog playing on the lawn. "I still don't understand what this has to do with Eliza."

"She made a comment about the tenants. Those born into privilege had an obligation to those who were not. Her words began a sort of introspection, and the more I remembered, the more depressed I became. I had wronged not only my husband but my son...and myself. I feared London because of the gossip about me, not your father. After Eliza came, I looked in the mirror and saw someone ugly who needed redemption." She held out her hands. "I am begging your forgiveness."

Nate turned, surprised at the vulnerability in his mother's eyes. His stomach twisted. "This is a shock, and I have much to think about."

"Yes, you do. But know this—I see an inner strength in Eliza that even she doesn't realize exists. When you propose marriage, and you will, the girl will turn you down thinking she is not good enough. Your father had little self-esteem being a third son with no exceptional talent. I destroyed what confidence he had left. If I had supported him, given him my strength to lean on, our lives might have been so different."

"I love her, Mother." He cursed then, remembering their last private conversation. "She's writing to relatives in Scotland, running away, I think."

"If she leaves, you will regret it. Eliza needs a man who realizes how remarkable she is, who will make *her* see how much she has to offer. And your return on that investment will be a future of hope and happiness." She clutched her son with a cold, slender hand. "Don't end up bitter and alone like your mother."

"Now hatred is by far the longest pleasure; men love in haste but they detest at leisure."

Lord Byron

Chapter Twelve

Early May
The Swine and Swig
Whitehall District, London

The tallow candles flickered as the heavy oak door opened, rusty iron hinges complaining against the violence of a sudden spring storm. Stale ale, unbathed bodies, and cheap perfume assaulted his nose as Landonshire stepped into the tavern. He scanned the dingy interior. The blackened beams above from a century of smoke, bodies crowded around the bar and the tables, and the proprietor's mongrel curled up by the hearth. A barmaid bent over to accept a coin from a customer, who slid his grimy fingers into her ample cleavage.

The place disgusted him, and he cursed Eliza for forcing him to patronize such an establishment if only for a quarter of an hour. He added another item to the list of reasons she'd suffer. No man should endure such indignities over a disobedient daughter. If it weren't for the marriage contract, he'd smash that beautiful face to a pulp. But Bellum didn't want a disfigured wife. Not for thirty thousand pounds.

In a corner by the fire, a man nodded at him. The marquess stood out in this crowd, his fine overcoat and hat worth more than a year's annual wage for some. He clutched the walking stick and fingered the hidden trigger that would produce a double-edged blade. One could never be too careful. He sat next to the shabby thief, noting the bawdy voices and slurred off-key serenade would cover any conversation he had at a tucked away table.

"What did you find out?" Landonshire didn't want to spend any more time here than necessary. His eyes burned from the poor ventilation and something had just scurried across his boot. "I'm not here to socialize."

"And 'ere I was goin' to offer ye a mug o' ale, milord," sneered the man. His once-blond hair, darkened by soot and grease, matched the stained and broken fingernails that tapped the rough-hewn table.

He held out a filthy hand. The marquess dropped a small leather bag into the palm, and the man wrapped his fingers around it with a grin then pushed it into his pocket.

"Now tell me, where is my daughter?"

"I went up to Sunderland, like ye said. She weren't at that castle, and she weren't at the Boldon place either. I was headed home, dejected ye see, 'cuz I was only goin' to get half the money since I couldn't find the girl. So I'm passing through this little village, Pendle, it was. I was hungry and they had a small inn there." He took a long pull of his ale and wiped his mouth with the back of his coat sleeve. "The barmaid there was a gabster. Of course, I can be very charmin' meself when I put me mind to it."

"Get on with it, or I'll take back the purse."

"Patience, milord," the man drawled, warming to his story. "I asked her if any strangers had passed through lately. Now she tells me of a footpad that got picked up by the constable a few weeks back. Tried to rob an old woman and then a fine coach that stopped to help. Seems a young woman of quality refused to give up the goods and took a whip to the cur." He waved his cup at the barmaid passing by.

"What does this have to do with my daughter?" Landonshire was ready to floor the weasel. He didn't have time for long tales.

"The young woman was blonde with a dark-haired little girl."

"How old was the child?"

"Two, maybe."

Landonshire grinned and rubbed his hands together. His winning horse was approaching the finish line. "And where did this young lady of quality go after that?"

"A local lord, Viscount Pendleton, brought the bully ruffian into the blacksmith and escorted the coach out of town. So I did some investigatin' and found there'd been some new guests at this gentleman's estate, Pendle Place." The man smiled, his gums glistening in the firelight.

"Go on."

"Lord Pendleton lives there with his mother and sister. But he's playin' the host to a young woman, pretty thing with golden hair and purple-like eyes.

The little girl is as dark as her mama is light. An older woman, round and slow-movin', watches over the youngster. The viscount is gone most of the day, so thought it'd be easy enough to snatch the little one. But she's got a dog watching over her, a scent hound. As soon as I got too close, he smelled me and started howling."

"Well done. If I need you again, I know where to find you." If he couldn't get the babe, he'd snatch Eliza. A week of "persuasion" would get her to say "I do" in front of a preacher. He would have enjoyed taunting the whore with the child. Ah well... Landonshire pulled his collar up and his hat down, turning his back on the man without another word. He headed out the door into the rain with a whistle on his lips.

*If I had a flower for every time I thought of you,
I could walk in my garden forever."*

Alfred Tennyson

Chapter Thirteen

*Mid-May
Pendle Place*

Eliza tipped her head back, enjoying the wind in her face and the smooth rhythm of the horse's canter. The sun peeked from behind huge, fluffy clouds that changed their shape as the wind pushed them along. Beside her, Nate rode his big bay gelding. The horse easily passed her smaller mare. Hannah had suggested a picnic on the river's bank. She rode behind them with a groom and the supplies for their outing.

Nate pulled up his horse and Eliza followed suit. He wore a deep blue riding coat that stretched across his broad shoulders. The tan breeches fit like one of her evening gloves, and she'd had to drag her eyes away from the sight of his muscular thighs gripping the saddle. Countless days riding the property with Maxwell had streaked his light brown hair with gold and bronzed his skin. He'd be "sinfully handsome" in one of her romantic novels.

"Have you heard from Grace or your relatives in Scotland?" he asked, reaching down to give his horse's neck a pat.

Eliza tore her eyes from his capable hands, remembering the touch of his long fingers against her skin, his thumb stroking her bottom lip. "No, not yet. They may ignore my request since we've never met, and my mother hasn't contacted them since she left. I'm counting on the relationship my aunt had with her family. It's presumptuous, at best, but I could think of no other way."

Leaving Pendle Place would break her heart. It had become a second home to Althea. They had both grown fond of Nathaniel and his family. And then there was Cyrano. How did you separate a girl and her faithful hound? They'd both be inconsolable for a time. *Oh Carson, am I making the right decision?*

"Good. The longer it takes, the more time I have with you."

He smiled. Her breath caught.

Those soft brown eyes, reflecting the gold of his hair, locked onto hers and held her gaze. They'd grown close over the last weeks. He made her feel special. She was not accustomed to a man asking her opinion, caring about what she read or enjoyed. It was a heady emotion, to feel significant, to feel as if one actually *mattered*.

The longer I stay the harder it will be to forget.

"You're flirting with me again," she said, hoping to curtail the fluttering wings in her belly.

"I won't stop. I warned you, didn't I?"

She laughed, a light genuine sound that had evolved over the last few weeks. Eliza barely recognized the sound as her own. The constant weight on her shoulders had lifted, though the nightmare of her mother still haunted her. "Yes, warned and duly noted. Hannah," she called over her shoulder, "did you have a place picked out or shall we look for a spot?"

"Keep going. It's just around the next bend near the woods. A place to enjoy the sun and shade for those of us avoiding freckles," she answered.

"I know the location. There's a nice grassy area with some flat rocks to spread out the food. Easy access to water the horses and several shade trees." Nate gathered his reins. "Shall we?" One eyebrow arched in question.

She grinned and instead of answering, smacked her horse with the crop and lunged ahead of him. He caught her easily but it didn't matter. Today, her heart was light and the day was perfect. By the time Hannah caught up with them, they had dismounted and spread a blanket on the ground.

Jagged rocks thrust out of the rushing clear water, an occasional fish emerging, its tail flapping before splashing under the fast-moving current. They walked the horses to the water's edge to drink then hobbled them under a tree to nibble at grass.

"Your mother has improved over the past few days. The color has returned to her cheeks," Eliza remarked as Hannah passed them each a cold beef pasty. "It's almost as if a burden has been lifted."

Nate coughed then sputtered. His sister pounded on his back while he caught his breath and reached for the flagon of lemonade. Wiping at his eyes, he shook his head. "I'm fine. Just a crumb stuck in my throat."

An hour went by, the trio lying on their back, quoting favorite lines of poetry, naming shapes from the clouds above. The day was perfect, the sky a brilliant cornflower blue, and she had a taste of what it felt like to be carefree. This is what she wanted for Althea. Eliza turned her head, studying the handsome profile next to her. That he was attached to her daughter, she was certain. That he was attracted to her, she had no doubt. But did he hold any stronger feelings? Did she?

Yes. She loved him. After sorting through her feelings, she realized he evoked a much stronger passion, a deeper need than with Carson. There had been so much gratitude in that bond. He'd treated her like a human being instead of property to be traded, sold, or used at will. She'd been thankful, but had grown emotionally since that time.

With Nathaniel, a hunger drove her to be near him, to close her eyes at the sound of his voice. Let his presence wash over her, stir her pulse, make her throb in those intimate places. Never seeing him again would burn a hole in her soul. And yet she must go. He was the type of man that once committed, his love professed, would never go back on his word. Eventually, he would recognize her for what she was. The pain of seeing regret in his eyes would keep her strong. They would leave as soon as she had word from Scotland.

"I'll pack up and send the groom on with the basket." Hannah rose and smoothed out her dress. "After I soak my feet in the river."

Eliza watched as Hannah removed her boots, picked up her skirts, and waded to the edge of the river. Far off to the west, dark clouds gathered, promising rain to come.

A scream startled her. Just off the shore, Hannah wobbled on the edge of a rock, lost her balance and fell. Nate jumped up, running for the river bank. His sister slapped at the water, swimming the short distance to the rock. A giggle rose above the splashing as she gripped at the stone and pulled herself back into the shallower water, collapsing on her bum. Nate reached her, held out a hand, and pulled up his dripping wet sister.

"I think I'll return earlier than planned." She picked up the hem of her dress, scrunched it up then wrung it out. A puddle formed beneath her, surrounding her stocking feet.

"Yes, we'll help gather everything and head back. You must get out of those clothes. Thank goodness it's a warm day." Eliza knew if a wind picked up, Hannah could still catch a chill.

"Oh no, stay. Why should all three of us sacrifice the rest of the afternoon because of my clumsiness?"

"I can't... We can't—"

"Of course you can. My brother may be a flirt, but he would never take advantage. And no one will be the wiser if you spend an hour without a chaperone." She grinned. "It's not like you're a young naïve miss in her first season. Gracious, you're a widow!"

"We wanted to show you the tree with the gruesome face in the trunk. It's so clear, as a child Hannah thought it could talk." Nate laughed. "She was furious when she found Maxwell hiding behind the tree."

"Oh yes, Eliza. You must see it. The face is like something from Merlin's tale." She laced up her boots. "It will take an hour or less. You'll be right behind me."

She agreed against her better judgment. As the pair rode away, Nate whispered in her ear, "Now I shall ravish the fair maiden!" He reached for her, giving her plenty of time to dash away. With a giggle, she escaped his arms and ran for the horses.

They retrieved their mounts and rode into the woods for a quarter of an hour. They stopped in front of an ancient oak, its twisted bark forming a misshapen face, complete with swirling eyes and a gaping hole for a mouth. A child could easily be convinced it was a magical tree.

"I see how Hannah was duped. This could be an illustration from *Grimm's Fairy Tales*." She moved the mare closer, bending down to rub her hand along the tree trunk. "We must bring Althea to see it."

A clap of thunder spooked Eliza's mare. She pulled back on the reins and murmured soothing words as she stroked its tense neck. The air was heavy with the threat of rain.

"Those clouds were moving faster than I thought," said Nathaniel. "Ready for a gallop?"

She nodded and they made their way back to the meadow. Just as they left the shelter of the woods, lightning ripped the sky and fat drops of rain began to fall.

"If it were only rain, I'd still say gallop back, but I hate to risk your safety in a storm." He pointed back at the woods. "We'll take shelter in the woodcutter's shed."

They moved as quickly as they could. Wind whipped leaves from the trees and sent the smaller wildlife scurrying for cover. The canopy of green provided some relief from the downpour but Eliza was still grateful to see the small cabin. Nate helped her from her horse, opened the door for her, then took the horses around back and tied them in a lean-to.

The cottage was one room, simply furnished, and dry. There was a small wooden table with two chairs, an oil lamp, a bed... *Pish and perdition!* She blushed at the sight of the small four-poster bed. The hearth was cold and dark with a stack of wood neatly piled next to it. A rocking chair faced the fireplace, and a thick fur rug lay in front of it. A small nightstand stood next to the bed with several books and a candle.

The door opened and Nate walked in, brushing the rain from his riding jacket. He peeled it off and placed on the back of one of the chairs. "I'll start a fire for us. Between the rain and the wind, I'm chilled. How are you?"

She nodded. "Cold and wet. This is a much better option than trying to beat the storm. There's a fine book selection, Grace stocked the place well." She fingered the leather-bound books of Blake, Cowper, and Tennyson. But it was *Pride and Prejudice* that she picked up and opened. Grace had sent her this book, the last one she'd read before leaving home and becoming a bride. Such romantic nonsense had filled her head.

"If I had a flower for every time I thought of you, I could walk in my garden forever," Nate quoted from behind her, his breath warm against her neck.

Eliza shivered from the nearness.

"Are you cold? The fire should heat this small room up quickly enough." He sat on the bed and took her hands, pulling her between his legs. He searched her face, a question in those beautiful eyes that had nothing to do with the temperature.

"You unnerve me at times," she replied honestly. "Yet I'm drawn to you like a moth to a flame. Trite, I know, but appropriate."

"That implies I could cause you harm." His jaw ticked, his grip tightening on her fingers. "I would never hurt you."

Her throat swelled. "No, but leaving this place will hurt, though I must go."

"Why?" One simple word, a question impossible for her to answer so he understood.

"I... I must secure a future for my daughter. Running from my father was a temporary solution. Lady Falsbury is right, I must find a way to keep us protected. Without sailing to America," she added with a sad smile.

Nate stood and pulled her close. She closed her eyes, his body warming the coldest corners of her heart. Why not enjoy this tenderness while she could? Why not be selfish for just this afternoon?

His head dipped, his mouth hovering above hers, their breath mingling. The room fell away, time suspended, and there was just his lips on hers. She closed her eyes and gave in to the passion, her arms sliding around his neck, fingers threading through his thick gold-streaked hair. He feathered kisses along her neck and she arched in response, her body molding to his, feeling his growing desire.

Nate pulled away then held her close, cradling her head on his shoulder. "Marry me," he whispered in her ear.

The beat of her heart grew so loud, she thought she'd misheard his words until he repeated them.

"Marry me, Eliza," he said louder. "Let me be a father to Althea and keep you safe forever."

"I-I..."

He tipped her chin up, his eyes soft with affection. "You care for me, I know. There is passion between us. If you don't love me yet, it will come. Many couples have begun with less."

Her chest tightened and she shook her head. "I care for you a great deal, which is why I cannot marry you." Turning away, she blinked back tears. Emotion would not help her now. *Be strong.* "I appreciate the kindness of your offer, though I could never subject you to such a life."

"Pardon me, but subject me to what? A life with a beautiful, gentle woman and her precocious, adorable child? Please God, strike me down now if there is a better fate for me." He cupped her face in his hands. "I love you, Eliza. I will marry you."

"You do not know me. A man of your standing requires a wife of potent character, of good breeding skilled in the social graces. A woman who does not flinch at an angry tone or draw back at an unexpected wave of a hand. You would come to regret your union with me."

"Never. Your family's title exceeds mine—"

"NO! I'm... I'm flawed, I'm tainted with my father's blood. My background is sordid and ugly." She pushed away from him and walked to the hearth. The crackling fire cast warmth into the room, but it did not reach her heart. It ached of having everything she'd dreamed of within in her reach and unable to snatch it. How could she make him understand she would never be his equal?

He stood behind her now, and Eliza longed to lean back into him, go back to where they had been a few hours ago. The chance to enjoy any intimacy with him was gone now. How those memories might have served her in the years to come. For this was the man she would love until her dying day. She knew it with the same certainty that she knew her father would never give up his quest for her.

"Why would the Falsburys, Kit, and Grace love and care for you so much if they thought you unworthy and 'tainted'? Your mother's blood, Graces' blood is in you as well. Good outweighs evil, don't you see?"

His hands stroked her arms, rubbing warmth into her as he spoke in a soft, soothing tone. Oh, how she wanted this man. Not only for herself but for Althea.

"Yes, they care for me and shelter me. They understand I am weak, someone who needs their strength and protection. You would grow tired of that. Why can you not see what they see?"

"In Lord Sunderland and Falsbury's defense, they have never seen you wield a whip. I have."

His fingers smoothed the hair back from her face and stroked it, leaving a trail of fire down her back. A tear slipped down her cheek, and she dashed it away. It would make him want to comfort her, and she felt herself giving in.

"Look at me, Eliza," he demanded as he turned her around to face him. He tilted her chin up. "You misinterpret fragility for weakness, flaws for scars. For one so well read, I should not have to explain the difference."

He cupped her face again, the pads of his thumbs stroking her skin, stoking the heat within her. If she looked into those kind, loving eyes, she would be lost and all resolve gone.

Nathaniel thought he would drown in a sea of violet. Her eyes sparkled with unshed tears and his jaw clenched, knowing he could not take away the agony of the past. But he could ensure no more pain marred their future.

"My mother said you would try to deny me. Because of you, she has come to terms with her own past. I've learned more about myself in the last few days than I have in my entire life."

He told her of the revelation of his father. The picture his mother had painted and he'd believed for so long. His misgivings and concerns that he would be like his father.

"In the end, we create our own person. We are who we strive to be and who those around us help us to be. Anyone can overcome their past with enough determination and support from loved ones. The key is allowing others to do that, to swallow our pride and lean on them when we need it. In return, they will lean on us one day."

"I had no idea I had any influence on Lady Pendleton, even indirectly." She bit her lip and peeked at him through her lashes. "But your father was no monster."

"No, he wasn't, but I was wounded all the same. Perhaps not physically but in here." He took her hand and laid it over his heart. "You are not weak but scarred. Terrible wounds do that. But the pain goes away and with time the scar fades. It may never totally disappear. I know that. But it will grow fainter as the years go by."

"A reminder of the past." He raised her hand to his lips and kissed her palm, never taking his eyes from hers. "An ugly reminder some days but also a beautiful remembrance of how much you've overcome."

His lips brushed over her trembling ones, tasted the sweetness, and dipped his head to claim her mouth. She stood still, not moving, not breathing. Then with a gasp, she threw her arms around him. Tears streamed down her cheek and mingled with their lips, a salty aphrodisiac that fed his desire.

"Don't give me an answer now. Instead, think over all I have said." He bent and kissed her again then feathered her neck with light kisses. "I'll say this and no more until you've heard from your relation."

She looked up at him, and he saw the hope in her eyes. The yearning to believe his words. "Remember this. I love you, Eliza. Lean on me now, so I may lean on you as we grow old together."

"The last act is bloody, however pleasant all the rest of the play is..."

Blaise Pascal

Chapter Fourteen

Mid May
Pendle Place

Landonshire had bided his time, knowing that perseverance and cleverness always prevailed. The situation was just as his paid mole had described Eliza's daily routine included a walk with her daughter after breakfast each day. The governess would collect her ward and the hound, then Eliza would spend time tending the plot of herbs. She'd always been a muttonhead that way, wanting to get her hands dirty and enjoying the outdoors.

Last Saturday had been quite a boon. Eliza had gone on a picnic with Pendleton and his sister. He'd watched the sister fall in the river and take her leave with the groom. Then Pendleton and Eliza had gone into the woods to look at some ridiculous tree. The storm hit and they had taken refuge in a cabin. The whore had stayed with the viscount until the storm had passed. Soaked to the bone, he'd waited until they left then entered the structure. It had been worth the chill to find this hideaway.

The little cabin presented the perfect hiding place for his plan. Bringing Eliza home would take too long. There would only be hours between the time he could snare his prey and Pendleton returned home. Falsbury and Sunderland could easily intercept him on the way. Instead, he'd sent his paid ruffian to escort Lady Landonshire here. He licked his lips, imagining her tied up on the bed of the deserted shed, her eyes wide with fright. His wife would be the cat's paw in this upcoming scene. Eliza would watch as he thrashed her mother. He'd learned some tricks over the years, ways to keep the blood flow down but heighten the pain. His blood heated thinking of the scene to come. The screams and groans of pain, the terror in their eyes, the pleas to stop. Mercy was not one of his virtues, he thought with a grin.

The staff was busy in other areas of the property this time of day but a stranger might attract attention. Noting the color and style of Pendleton's coat and horse each morning, Landonshire had used the last of his blunt to purchase similar items. His own mount had grown long in the tooth, so he'd had to spend more than anticipated and throw in his pocket watch. But if someone spotted him riding along the back of the property, they would think it was the master returning home.

This morning he'd been careful to keep a safe distance upwind from the gardens, so the hound wouldn't catch an unfamiliar scent and tip off any of the groundskeepers. Watching the older woman walk away with the girl and hound, he chuckled at his granddaughter holding the dog's ear as if it were

a hand. She was a pretty little thing. If he could get her away from Falsbury, she might be worth something to him one day.

Too bad about the viscount. After seeing their romantic tryst, Landonshire almost had a pang of sympathy for his daughter. If her next husband didn't linger too long, and Pendleton remained a bachelor, they could marry then. He would have his thirty thousand, Bellum would have had his heir, and who cared what the little whore did after that.

With a shrug, he dug the sharp spur into his stallion's flank, drawing blood and sending the beast lunging down the hill. It was time to collect the merchandise.

Eliza knelt in the herb plot and pulled a weed away from the rosemary. The garden was therapeutic. Watching the new growth, tending the soil, inhaling the spicy scent of herbs was a balm in itself. She could clear her mind and think while she tended the herbs. And there was so much to think about. Marriage. Nathaniel. A family. Was his love genuine or only an infatuation with the woman he thought her to be? Oh, how she wanted to stay at Pendle Place, marry this wonderful man, and live happily ever after.

Black boots appeared on one side of her. Nate! He'd come back early. A hand pulled back her hair and she smiled. Then fingers dug into her skull, grabbed a handful of hair, and snapped her head back. She stared into the face of her father. *Nooo!*

"Good morning, my sweet daughter. I've missed you." His other hand covered her mouth. "Let's not be too loud in our excitement in being reunited, eh?

I have a pistol, and anyone who tries to stop us will find out what a good shot I am. Do you understand?"

She nodded, eyes wide and body trembling. *Show no fear. Show no fear.* He fed on it and grew stronger. Eliza would not give him more power. *Breathe in...and out. In...and out.* Her mind calmed. *Now think!*

He slowly removed his hand from her mouth. "We're going for a little ride. Your mother is anxious to see you."

Mama? Oh God, what had he done to her mother? "You're taking me home?" Falsbury or Sunderland would find her there. They might even be able to catch them if she found a way to slow down their progress. But the next words sent a chill down her spine.

"I like the little haven of love you and Pendleton visited the other day. Deserted, rarely used. We'll have plenty of privacy while we...talk." He yanked her hair again and pulled her from the garden plot onto the stone path. "I'm sure you remember how I love to talk."

He'd been watching them? A tremor passed through her body. "Mama is there?" *Think! Think! Think!* Her hands scraped along the small rocks as he dragged her backward, pain scorching the back of her scalp. The cabin was less than an hour's ride. How could she let Nathaniel know where they would be? *Cyrano.* She had to distract her father, give him what he wanted.

"Yes, she's waiting for you. We'll have a lovely reunion, just like old times, yes?"

"Papa, I'm s-so s-sorry. Please don't hurt me."

A malicious grin widened his face. Meeting his gaze, she pleaded with him. Her stomach twisted as the familiar glee glittered in his eyes. Her fingers dug into the pebbles beneath her, clutching at as many as she could against her palm and sliding one hand into the pocket of her skirt.

"I will do whatever you say, just don't hurt Althea."

"I wanted her but that noisy hound never leaves her side. But I'm a resourceful man."

She slid the other handful of pebbles into the opposite pocket. Just as she attempted another fistful, he hauled her to her feet. He took her hand and began to pull her toward the back of the garden. Hopping behind him for a few steps, she pulled her thin leather shoe off and dropped it. Then she dragged the toe of her other shoe along the ground as much as possible without Landonshire's notice.

He said they were going for a ride. A carriage or even a curricle would be noticed, so they would be on horseback. Once she was off the ground, she would have to drop enough items along the way to keep Cyrano tracking the scent. She prayed the pebbles would be enough.

"Shall I hold you in front of me or will you behave? Remember, I have a pistol"—he patted a bulge under his waistcoat—"and I'll shoot anyone who follows us. I'm a desperate man with little left to lose but a great deal to gain."

The thought of his arms around her, his breath heavy against her head, sent bile rushing up her throat. "Behind." When he turned to mount the horse, she pulled the two ribbons from her hair and slid them inside her gloves. That would give her four pieces of material to drop as well as the stones. She prayed it would be enough.

The stallion had a smooth gallop and she was able to hold on with one hand most of the journey. Landonshire assumed she wanted as little contact with him as possible. She'd dropped her last item, a glove, at the entrance of the woods and hoped it would be enough. The day was clear with little wind. Eliza didn't know if that was better for Cyrano or not.

They reached the cabin and tears pricked the backs of her eyes. The recurring nightmare. Oh, God. Her father pulled her off the horse, grabbed her wrists, and pulled her inside. Mama lay curled on the bed, her ankles and wrists bound, a handkerchief stuffed in her mouth. Holding back a sob, she noted her mother's hair had turned completely gray. The lines on her face had deepened and new wrinkles appeared. Her cheek was swollen and bruised. But she was alive.

"Mama, oh Mama."

Her mother's eyes grew wide, tears shining as she shook her head.

"Isn't this nice? My two favorite girls together again." He bent over his wife, kissed her forehead, and pushed her off the bed. She landed with a hard *thump* on her side and a cry of pain.

She rushed to her mother's side. When Eliza touched her mother's hip, the older woman gave her a determined look and an almost imperceptible shake of the head. Eliza understood. Backing away, she sank onto one of the chairs. Her mother would not play the role of a victim. Not today.

"What, no tearful reunion? We can change that soon enough." He took off his coat and laid it carefully over the other chair. "I'm a bit tired. Your mother was escorted here under the cover of darkness so I rose quite early this morning."

He went to a corner behind the door and retrieved more rope. With a sinking heart, Eliza saw their last hope of escape disappear. *Breathe in...and out. In...and out.* If she lost her wits, their chance of survival would disappear as well. And they would survive, by God. He would not win.

"I apologize for not playing the host, but I do need a nap," he said, his tone conversational as if discussing which parlor game to play after supper. He seized her wrists, tied them together, and tied her ankles to the chair legs. Pulling a handkerchief from his pocket, he held it out. "Open up, my dear. I need utter silence while I sleep."

Eliza stared at him, her mouth clamped tight. He laughed, walked over to his wife, and kicked her in the stomach. He pulled his foot back and aimed for her head.

"No!"

He nodded. "That's my girl. Now let's try this again." He stood in front of her again. "Open wide," he taunted and shoved the cloth into her mouth. A corner of it lay on the back of her tongue and she thought she would choke. But it dampened and the gagging ceased.

Landonshire removed his cravat and pistol and placed them both on the table. Then he untied his shirt, kicked off his boots, and lay on the bed. Within minutes, his light snore floated across the room. Eliza and her mother locked eyes, and one lone tear slipped down the bruised cheek.

The sun could not be seen from inside the cabin, so they had no idea how much time had passed. He woke with a snort and a snarl, looking around the room confused. A smile curled his lips as he remembered where he was.

"Anyone hungry? No? I have some bread and cheese and a flask of wine." He retrieved the saddle bag from beside the bed. Rummaging through it, he pulled out bread and cheese wrapped in brown paper and a flat metal container. He took a bite of cheese and chewed slowly.

"Oh my love, I bet you haven't eaten since supper last night. That's too bad." He tore off a chunk of the bread. "You *have* become a little thick in the middle."

He finished off the bread and wrapped the rest of the cheese in the butcher paper. "Now, shall we get straight to business?"

He stood and tied the strings of his shirt together. Then he retrieved a leather glove from his coat. Pulling it over his hand, he clutched the hair on the top of his wife's head with his bare fingers and lifted her half off the ground. With his gloved hand, he punched her in the side of the face.

"What, no sound? Ah, playing the martyr for our daughter. The maternal sacrifice is endearing." His next blow came to the stomach, and he grinned as a low muffled moan escaped. "You see, Eliza, the key to persuasion is making sure that your opponent never loses consciousness. I've grown quite skilled at this. I can judge by the eyes if it's close and allow a little time for recuperation." He released her hair, and she crumpled to the ground.

"Not everyone has the same tolerance for pain. Others acquire it along the way. You, for example, were never able to withstand much. While your mother has become very tolerant of it." He leaned over and backhanded his wife, her head thumping against the floorboards.

Eliza struggled, pulling at the bindings. Her stomach roiled. If she vomited with the cloth in her mouth, she would surely choke. Every muscle in her body tensed as her father inflicted blow after blow on his wife. Her nightmare had become reality. She blinked, fighting the tears, knowing her mother would sacrifice herself to save her daughter.

And then he began to sing. The words of *Amazing Grace* echoed against the timber walls. He'd lost his mind. Oh, no. If he were insane, there would be no escape. Perhaps he'd only brought her here to kill them both. Then the serenade stopped as quickly as it had begun.

The fiend untied her ankles and removed the handkerchief from her mouth. Eliza gasped, sucking in air that made her cough against the dryness of her mouth and throat. A shared look of horror passed between mother and daughter as the grinning demon untied his second captive and pulled off the gag. They knew Landonshire enjoyed watching them struggle, kick and flail against the beatings. And now he wanted to hear them beg for mercy.

"So tell me, Eliza, what are your plans for the future?" he asked in a friendly tone. "Are you ready to settle down again?"

She stared at him, her tongue frozen, her mind whirling. What did he want her to say? If she agreed to his demands too soon, they might leave before Nathaniel had time to find them. If she did not, her mother could die.

"What if I refuse to say the words at the wedding?"

"That was anticipated, my dear. Bellum searched out a minister who's short on brass and practically deaf. Once the contract is signed, he will be witness that you are legally bound."

"I-I would prefer a younger man," she croaked out, her throat parched and her tongue thick from the handkerchief.

"Ha! The little whore wants a younger man. I cannot seem to please you."

He pulled the rocker away from the fireplace and set it next to his wife. He sat down and tipped the chair back on its curved legs and grabbed the heavy iron poker.

"First"—he jabbed the end of the poker into his wife's thigh—"I give you a young, rich husband." With the toe of his foot, he pushed at the small circle of blood forming through her dress.

"Father, please," moaned Eliza. How could her mother not make a sound? Her eyes stayed focused on her daughter, as if Eliza were her life's blood.

"Shut your mouth while I'm speaking!" He jabbed his wife's other thigh. "That impudent young whelp refused to invest in one of my ventures. Well, we know what happens when I'm crossed, don't we? He shouldn't have done that."

Cold terror filled Eliza's gut. Her hands trembled against the ropes, and she fought for breath. *Carson? He killed Carson?*

"Ah, you *do* understand! It was a shame because that *accident* could have easily been avoided."

"Murderer! You murdered Carson, you blasted devil!" His evil had no bounds. He'd always been a monster but to arrange to have her husband killed. And Nathaniel could be on his way. Her heart in shreds, her stomach churning, her blood boiling, the rage took over. Oh, to scrape that smug look off his face. She eyed the pistol on the table. Or shoot it off his face.

That would end it. If Landonshire was dead, she would be free. One look at her mother, and it would be obvious they had been defending themselves. She inched toward the gun.

"Listen to your daughter." Landonshire shook his head and bent to pat his wife's cheek then squeezed it, twisting the skin between his thumb and two fingers.

Eliza reached for the pistol. Her hands wrapped around its handle but the binds on her wrists made handling it awkward. She got her finger onto the trigger but struggled to pull back the hammer.

"What the bloody hell do you think you're doing?"

He jumped from the rocker and charged at her. Eliza fought to pull back the hammer but couldn't get her thumbs in position. His hand grabbed her wrist as they grappled for the flintlock. Landonshire bent her wrist back, and the gun flew from her hand. It hit the floor and slid across the wood, stopping in front of her mother's face. She watched the look come over the older woman's features and knew they both had the same thought.

Eliza clutched her father's shirt and screamed at him, anticipating the blow that flung her head against the back of the chair. She reached up and scratched his face, prepared for his wrath while her mother picked up the gun. The hammer clicked and the room fell silent. Its occupants went still. In the distance came the low bay of a hound.

"Cowards die many times before their deaths; the valiant never taste of death but once."

William Shakespeare

Chapter Fifteen

Sheep Shed
Pendle Place

The sheep bleated, fear and irritation showing in the whites of its eyes. The farmer made quick use of his blades, peeling the wool off and tossing it onto a growing pile. Finished, he released the mewling sheep and it ran pell-mell from the shed. Nate had been pleased with the wool business this year. It was turning a profit and providing work for his tenants. Gideon had told him on the last visit that his textile business would continue to buy all the wool he could produce.

"Here comes Mr. Maxwell." The farmer nodded his head toward the open door. A horse and rider appeared at the top of a distant hill, riding at breakneck speed.

His chest tightened. Only an emergency would provoke his steward to approach in such haste. "I must go. Excellent work" He rushed outside and untied his gelding. Could it be Mother? He met Maxwell at the bottom of the hill. The man was in a sweat and his horse's neck glistened from exertion.

"Lady Hannah sent me. Lady Eliza is gone. She found a shoe in the garden but the lady herself is nowhere on the grounds."

For a moment, Nate could not move. An unfamiliar terror gripped his muscles. Then Maxwell spurred him into action.

"She's afraid Landonshire has taken her."

"Hiya!" Nathaniel applied crop and heel to his horse and they galloped up the hill. By Christ, he'd kill the man.

At Pendle Place, his mother and sister had ordered fresh horses readied for both men. The ladies faces were grim as they waited, Cyrano patiently lying at their feet. His manservant stood behind them holding two pistols. "Ready and loaded, my lord," he said as he handed them over.

"The post brought news from Grace today," began Hannah. "I went to find Eliza, knowing she would want to read the letter right away. I found this." She handed the shoe to her brother.

Lady Pendleton's voice was brisk and in charge. "I've sent for Dr. Goodman. He's in the next village and should arrive within a few hours. I also posted a quick note to Sunderland Castle."

"Thank you." Nate tucked one of the pistols into his saddlebag and handed the second to Maxwell. "I will bring her home. I promise you that." If it took his last dying breath.

"I know you will, son." She placed a hand on his boot and looked up at him, sorrow darkening her eyes. "Now off with you both, there is no time to waste."

With a whistle, Cyrano followed the men to the spot where the shoe had been found. The disturbed gravel bore witness to the struggle that had occurred. Eliza had not gone willingly. An invisible knife twisted in Nate's gut. His fists clenched and unclenched in raw fury. "If he's harmed one hair on her head, I *will* kill him."

He dismounted and held the shoe to the hound's nose. The canine sniffed the item at length, put his nose in the air, and then to the ground. With a deep bay, Cyrano padded off, his ears dragging along the pebbled path.

"Send a wagon after us. We may need it for..." Nate's voice trailed off, his jaw clenched.

Maxwell reached out and gripped his shoulder. "She hasn't been gone long, a couple hours at most. We'll find her."

The dog stopped at the edge of the field. "This must be where they mounted." Nathaniel swallowed. What if they couldn't pick up a scent? They'd never find her if they didn't know what direction Landonshire had taken.

Cyrano circled a wide area several times, put his nose in the air again, and circled once more. With a mournful howl, he set off toward the river, intent on a familiar scent.

"He's got it!" cried Maxwell. Peering down at the spot the dog had sniffed so enthusiastically, he pointed. "Look, pebbles. The same type from the garden path."

Nate let out the breath he'd been holding. "God's bones, she's left a trail."

"Clever girl," the steward said. "Now let's see how far we can follow it."

They came upon a stream and found a pale blue ribbon on the other side. When they had to jump a small ditch, a glove had been left to mark the direction. *I'm coming, love. Stay strong.* If he could give the canine wings, he would. Every minute could be another blow of pain to Eliza. His fingers squeezed the reins, his knuckles white.

As the trio came upon the picnic spot, dread filled Nate's belly. How long had the marquess been watching them? His suspicions were confirmed when a final ribbon lay at the entrance of the woods.

"Bloody hell, she's at the woodcutter's shed." He spurred the gelding, and they cantered into the shade, Cyrano sprinting behind, his bay echoing against the trees trunks.

Nathaniel was off the horse before it came to a stop. From inside the shed, they heard a scream and then a female voice shouted, "I'll see you in hell!"

"I'm not going alone, you ungrateful whore." *Landonshire!*

A grim smile curved Nathaniel's lips as he realized his avenging angel had returned to him. He retrieved the pistol from his saddlebag and pulled the hammer back, fully cocked. Maxwell kicked open the door, wood splintering under the force of his boot, and both men entered, pistols raised. As Nate's eyes adjusted to the light, a horrific scene unfolded before him.

Eliza sat on a chair, her wrists bound; Landonshire held a knife to her throat while his wife aimed a pistol at her husband's chest. A trio of long bloody scratches marred his left cheek.

Then all hell broke loose.

Their entrance had distracted the marquess. As he turned, the knife scraped Eliza's skin, blood oozing from the cut. Lady Landonshire shrieked. A pistol shot reverberated against the timber walls, and Landonshire stumbled but stayed upright.

"You shot me!" he yelled in fury. His hand went to his chest. He stared in disbelief at the blood dripping from his fingers. "You'll both pay for that." He raised his arm, the knife point aimed at Eliza.

Nate pulled the trigger. The second shot hit Landonshire squarely in the forehead. He wavered for a moment, mouth slack, eyes in shock, then collapsed in a dull crash.

Nathaniel dropped the flintlock and ran to Eliza, scooped her in his arms, and rocked her back and forth. She sobbed, gasping for breath and clutching at his jacket. "Shhh, it's all right. I have you. You're safe. Your mother is safe." He kissed the top of her head and continued to murmur soft words in her ear until she calmed.

Maxwell carried Lady Landonshire to the bed and gently laid her on the counterpane. She whimpered at each movement, and the steward cursed as he tried to tend her wounds. He pulled a knife from his belt and cut the rope binding her wrists then did the same for her daughter.

Returning to the bed, he said gently, "I apologize, my lady, but I need to raise the hem of your dress and stop the bleeding from your thighs." He removed his cravat and tore it in half. She nodded and emitted a quiet moan as he applied pressure to the punctures in her legs. "Hold these if you can, my lady, and I'll fetch some cold water."

She nodded and smiled weakly. "My daughter?"

"I'm fine, Mama. Please do as he asks," Eliza acknowledged from across the room.

Her voice was weak but clear and Nathaniel whispered a silent prayer. "Yes, let's get you cleaned up also."

Maxwell returned with a bucket of water from the well. Using the handkerchief that had been her gag, Nate wiped the blood from Eliza's neck.

"Is he..."

He nodded. "He won't ever hurt you again."

"Please, help my mother. She's much worse than I am and has lost too much blood."

He nodded but didn't move. Relief seeped through him like honey, sweet and satisfying. She was in his arms again, and he was reluctant to let her go. But the dead man next to him, lying in a puddle of blood, assured him that she was safe.

Eliza touched his cheek. "Thank you," she whispered and went slack in his arms.

"She fainted," Nate announced.

"It has been a trying day," agreed Maxwell. He turned to the marchioness. "A wagon is on its way. I'm afraid the ride back will not be pleasant for you."

"My dear sir, the bumpiest of wagons could not compare to the trials I have been through. Do not worry yourself on that account." Pain threaded her voice but her blue eyes were clear. "Today I have been emancipated. I can bear a bit more discomfort."

Nathaniel nodded at his future mother-in-law. A howl outside alerted them to the arrival of the

wagon. He rose, adjusting Eliza in his arms. She was alive. That was all that mattered. And today would be the first day of the rest of their lives.

Eliza leaned against the wagon seat, absorbing every rut and jostle of the wagon, her mother's head cushioned in her lap. A blanket covered Lady Landonshire, and she clutched it as her teeth chattered.

"I think a fever is coming on," Eliza said aloud to Nathaniel, who sat above her on the bench. "Please don't let her die."

A strong hand grasped her shoulder, lending warmth to the chill that overtook her own body. "I will do everything in my power, love. I'm going as fast as possible. We don't want to do more harm getting you both back to Pendle Place. Maxwell went ahead to prepare the household."

She nodded then gave a grateful smile to the groom, following behind the wagon leading Nathaniel's mount. Taking a deep, steadying breath, Eliza wondered how the day could appear so fine when a man lay dead. Birds chirped, a stray hawk swooped down over a field and rose up with a rodent in its beak. The stream below gurgled as the sun glinted off the water, making it sparkle and shine. The scent of freshly cut hay floated on the air from a nearby field. A day like any other except... They were free. Grief would not take hold of her heart.

Eliza stroked her mother's hair, her prone body jerking with the motion of the wagon. "We no longer have anything to fear, Mama. We are finally safe."

She closed her eyes, gave in to her emotions, and allowed the silent tears to wash away her sorrow. Not for her father, never for him. Sorrow for the pain they had been dealt, for the time they had lost, for the unfairness of it all. Life would go on, as it always had, but this time with hope. With the tears came a fresh start, a new life.

─────

"I'll take Eliza to her room. Maxwell, please follow my mother and carry Lady Landonshire to the guest quarters."

She woke to the rumble of Nathaniel's deep commanding voice against her cheek. She was in his arms, her head cradled on his chest, and could feel the urgent movement around her, even with her eyes closed.

"I'll need clean strips for bandages and hot water for..." Dr. Goodman called out to someone as his voice drifted away.

How had she fallen asleep? Eliza wondered as she struggled to open her eyes. When her lids finally obeyed, golden brown eyes, darkened by concern, greeted her.

"Rest, my love. We're home and I'm taking you upstairs." Nate kissed the top of her head. "When you wake, I'll tell you and Thea a story about an avenging angel who slayed a devil."

She smiled at the word *home*, and the world went dark again.

Eliza's head pounded when she tried to open her eyes so she kept them closed. The pillow under her was solid, as hard as... Her lids flew open to find she was tucked against Nathaniel, his arm tightening around her protectively, her knee resting on his hard thigh.

"How do you feel?" He brushed her hair away from her face and looked down at her. "Hungry?"

She shook her head. The waning afternoon light cast shadows across the four-poster bed, the curtains from an open window fluttering softly in the breeze. "My mother..." Her voice faltered.

"Is doing as well as can be expected, considering the beating she took. Several broken ribs but her jaw is only bruised, not cracked." He rolled slightly to his side and pulled her closer. "Dr. Goodman is amazed at what your mother endured. But as long as we prevent any infection to her puncture wounds, he feels she'll make a full recovery. I see now where your strength comes from."

Strength. Was that truly what she and her mother possessed? Eliza had always considered herself stubborn with a dogged determination to survive. Did that make her strong? Perhaps. Perhaps her weakness had been not acknowledging her own power and abilities.

"I cannot mourn his passing after all he's done. I don't have any tears left to shed for him." She pushed herself onto an elbow and looked at the man beside her. "You saved our lives."

"No," he said with a smile. "If I'm being truthful, Cyrano is the hero but only after your quick thinking. Dropping those stones with your scent..." He shook his head. "I never would have found you at the woodcutter's shed."

Gently, he disengaged his arm, shook it vigorously, and gave her a sheepish grin. When he moved forward, she panicked and clutched at his sleeve. Heat rose up her neck, increasing the pounding in her head. Tears of shame burned her eyes as she pulled his arm back. "Don't go yet."

He chuckled. "Not to worry, my love. You will be hard pressed to get rid of me." He tenderly kissed her forehead and then each eye, his lips warming her skin and sending her pulse into a frenzy. "I thought we'd sit up so you could take a drink."

Feeling foolish, she sipped at the lemony liquid. Her hand went to her hair, and she blushed again when her fingers touched the mass of tangles. "I must look a fright."

"You are the most beautiful sight I could wish for." He tipped her chin and brushed her lips. "I thought my heart would stop when I'd learned you were missing. I'd have given my life to keep you from him."

Yes, she thought, he truly would have. He would do anything for her or Althea or her mother. He was that kind of a man. The kind of man she could love without fear. The kind of man who would let her be herself—no, find herself—and enjoy the discovery with her, by her side.

"How is Althea?" she asked. What had her daughter seen or been told? Her heart ached for Thea, worried she'd been witness to their bloody return.

"Blissfully ignorant of the whole event. Mrs. Watkins kept her out of earshot when we arrived. She told her that Lady Landonshire had had an accident on her way here and you were both resting." He gave her a squeeze, and the familiar gesture made her heart swell. "I can't guarantee how long we'll keep her at bay, though. She's a bit like her mother when she's determined."

"Thank you," she whispered. She reached for his hand cradling her cheek and kissed the palm. "Thank you for..."

For what? How could she put into words what he had done for her? How did she thank him for mending the crack in her heart, bringing light to her darkness, turning her sorrow and fears into hope?

"I think fate has been on my shoulder since I first saw you cracking that whip. I've only played my part in the destiny already decided for us. No reason to thank me." He winked. "How are you feeling?"

She reached up and traced the line of his jaw, rubbed her thumb across his full lower lip, and smiled. "A bit sore, my head aches, but for the first time in my life, I feel...whole. I owe you so much."

"The only repayment I need is to have you and your mother happy and well. Speaking of which, do you think you could eat something for me? I can have tea and a cold repast brought up. Althea may join us if you like."

Eliza hesitated. Here they were, in bed together as a man and wife might be, and she had rebuked his offer of marriage. Well, she hadn't accepted. What if he'd changed his mind? She couldn't blame him. Yet, would he be lying here with her if he had?

"Nathaniel, I want you to know that whatever happens in the future—"

"Hush. We won't speak of the future until you are well. Just know this. My feelings have not changed." He kissed her then, their lips melting together, his fingers trailing her jawline down to her neck.

Just love me, Nate. Just love me, please.

And with a sigh and a smile, she gave in to his caresses. There would be little she could ever deny this man.

"Nothing contributes so much to tranquilize the mind as a steady purpose – a point on which the soul may fix its intellectual eye."

Mary Shelley

Chapter Sixteen

Two days later
Pendle Place

"The Justice of the Peace has arrived, my lord," announced the butler.

"Show him in, please. And inform Lady Eliza I will meet her in the library in one hour." Nathaniel ran a hand through his hair and let out a long breath. "I'd like to keep the women out of this if possible."

Maxwell nodded. "It's fortunate the good doctor here was able to take care of the autopsy. Hopefully we can close this investigation today."

The JP entered the room. All three men rose to greet him. "Sit, gentlemen, sit. I am sorry to see all of you under such grim circumstances. Let's dispense with the niceties and get right to the matter, shall we?" The elderly man set his satchel on his lap after he settled into a chair. He pulled out some papers, adjusted his spectacles, and raised a wrinkled face to his audience.

"The body is in the carriage house, and we can bring you to the scene of the crime if necessary. It's a small woodcutter's shed on my property."

"We'll see after I hear the testimony," he said, pale brown eyes focusing on Nathaniel. "You may begin."

Nate explained the background, Landonshire's abuse, attempts to coerce his daughter into marriage, and then the kidnapping. "When I arrived at the cabin, he had a knife raised in the air ready to strike Lady Eliza and scratches down his face. It seemed she had fought him at one point, and he was retaliating. When he saw me, I gauged by the crazed look in his eye that he would not see reason, though we tried."

"So you feel the marquess would have harmed his daughter?" asked the JP as he dipped his pen in the ink bottle and scratched more notes. "You felt the need to intervene in the defense of another?"

"Yes, the brute was out of control. When he aimed the blade for Lady Eliza, I shot him." Nate gave Maxwell a side-glance. "Twice."

Dr. Goodman agreed. "Yes, the body had one shot to the chest and another to the head."

"So you had to shoot him more than once?" asked the man, adjusting his glasses as he looked up at Nathaniel.

"He was...a difficult man to stop, large of build and in excellent shape for his age."

"I understand. And the weapon type?"

"One of Manton's tube lock double-barreled pistols. I picked it up in London last year."

The little man itched his bald pate with the tip of his pen and looked to the physician for confirmation. The doctor nodded his agreement.

"And the ladies? May I get a statement from them?"

Nathaniel glanced at Maxwell before speaking. "I would prefer we handle this without involving the women. Unless you wouldn't mind waiting another week or so? They are recuperating from the tragedy, and Lady Landonshire is in a great deal of pain."

Dr. Goodman added to this sentiment. "The marchioness has punctures in both thighs, a concussion at best, and is extremely weak at this point."

The JP shook his head. "No, I think with your testimony, and Dr. Goodman being so kind to step in as coroner, this should be sufficient. Mr. Maxwell, do you agree with Lord Pendleton's summary of events?"

"I do."

"Then I'd like to finish up this nasty business as soon as possible." He collected his notes, placed them in his worn leather satchel, and rose. "Please give my condolences to the ladies. I will be in touch, but I see no reason for a formal hearing."

Nathaniel paced up and down the Axminster carpet, anxious to begin his new life. *Their* new life. Eliza entered, bruised and beautiful, in his favorite blue gown marked with tiny purple flowers and pink satin ribbons. The colors matched her swollen eye. He smiled as she dipped her head, trying to hide the injury. Her blonde hair was pulled up into a bun but waves of golden tresses caressed her skin and were somewhat effective at covering a cut on her cheek. Long white gloves hid the scratches on her forearms and the raw skin around her wrists.

"You are lovely regardless of any physical mark"—he held out his arms and she stepped into them—"or invisible one."

She looked up, long pale lashes creating shadowed crescents upon her cheek, and gave him a bittersweet smile. "I may sound melancholy, but I wish this could have ended well. So much violence, so many regrets…"

"I have spoken with the Justice of the Peace and he is satisfied. There will be no need for you or your mother to endure a trial. I killed the Marquess of Landonshire in defense of you and your mother."

"But my mother—"

"Is recuperating and neither of you deserve the trauma of reliving the sordid details." He pulled her close and kissed the top of her head, taking in that. "Now, what did the letter from Grace say?"

"My relatives would welcome the chance to get know Althea and me. I am to write them at my convenience with my plans." She spoke into his chest, her words muffled.

He tipped up her chin and brushed a lock of blonde silk behind her ear. "And do you want to go to Scotland?"

Eliza shook her head but would not meet his eyes. He bent on one knee, brought one gloved hand to his lips. "Eliza, I ask you again with all the sincerity of a gentleman in love. Will you be my wife?"

A tear slid down her cheek. She brushed it away, nodded her head, and gave him a watery smile. "Yes, Nathaniel Pendleton. With all the sincerity of a lady in love, yes."

He stood and gathered her in his arms. His lips brushed hers softly until her arms slid around his neck. Her soft form, molded against his, his need roaring through his veins. His mouth claimed hers, his hands caressing every curve, every soft hollow. His lips trailed down her neck and over her shoulders while passion pulsed through his core. Pulling back just enough to speak, he bent his forehead to hers, trying to control his growing desire. Their breaths mingling, his voice husky as he whispered, "I will protect your mother and daughter and help you heal. I will be with you each day while you grow stronger and marvel at the woman you are and the woman you will become. I love you, Eliza, with every breath in my body."

"Look back, and smile on perils past."

Walter Scott

Epilogue

Pendle Place
Two weeks later

"Stop hovering over me, daughter. I am fine." Lady Landonshire stood next to her bed, clutching the back of a chair. "My legs won't get any stronger lying in bed."

"It's only been two weeks, Mama. You aren't recovered yet."

"Dr. Goodman said I could get out of bed whenever I thought myself ready. I'm ready." Her mother's chin stuck out, indicating the conversation was over.

With a sigh, Eliza resigned herself. Her mother had withstood so much. It was hard to believe her father was dead and they were all safe. And she was betrothed. The banns would be read next month after they were sure Lady Landonshire was well enough to attend the ceremony. She would meet her relatives from Scotland for the first time when they arrived for the wedding.

After hobbling about the room once, the older woman returned to her bed. "That's enough for one day. I don't want to tire myself before Grace and Lord Sunderland arrive tomorrow."

"Did I tell you the Falsburys will be here soon? I know they miss Althea terribly, as we miss them. They should arrive some time in the next two weeks. I do wonder what they will think of their granddaughter's new companion."

Her mother shuddered. "That drooling beast! But he is so devoted to our little girl. And he is a hero of sorts, I suppose."

Hearing a knock on the door, the women turned to find Hannah with a tray of tea. Nate stood beside her, holding Althea's hand, who in turn held Cyrano's ear. "May we come in?"

"Of course. I just finished a bit of exercise and need to rest. The company would be lovely. Come give me a kiss, Althea."

The little girl ran to the bed and pulled herself up to sit next to her grandmother. She very carefully leaned over and kissed Lady Landonshire on the good cheek. Hannah poured the tea for everyone and settled in a chair at the foot of the bed. Eliza sat next to Nate, trying to wipe the smile off her face. It happened every time he entered a room. He was a hero, her hero. No romantic novel could have created a man more wonderful than Viscount Pendleton.

The inquiry by the Justice of the Peace had been handled by Nathaniel. Dr. Goodman had taken the place of a coroner. Nate had taken responsibility for Landonshire's death with Maxwell as the witness.

That act alone had convinced Eliza that he would do everything in his power to keep her and her family safe. *Their* family safe.

When he proposed again, she'd remembered what he'd said in the cabin, while the storm raged outside and he had captured her heart.

You are not weak but scarred. Terrible wounds do that. But the pain goes away and with time the scar fades. It may never totally disappear. I know that. But it will grow fainter as the years go by.

Eliza repeated those words every day. It had become part of her morning ritual. And she came closer to believing it each time.

"Have you given any more thought to our proposal, Lady Landonshire?" asked Nathaniel. He tried to look around Althea, who now sat on his lap, busy trying to retie his cravat.

"I believe I will accept your offer. There is nothing that could make me happier than spending my final days with grandchildren surrounding me." Her eyes shone. "The dowager's house will be a piece of heaven for me. I can't thank you enough."

He shook his head and picked up Eliza's hand. "No, my lady, I can't thank you enough."

Eliza breathed in deeply. The carriage of life would still have unexpected turns. But these days, she held onto that leather strap with joy and anticipation.

Reviews are the life's blood of any author. If you enjoyed this book, please consider leaving a review at your favorite retailers.

Sneak Peek

Rhapsody and Rebellion
(Once Upon a Widow #3)

The story of Gideon, Earl of Stanfeld, and the
Highland beauty Alisabeth MacNaughton

"Those who dream by day are cognizant of many things which escape those who dream only by night."

Edgar Allen Poe

Chapter One

August 16, 1819
Stanfeld Estate,
County of Norfolk, England

Gideon touched the horse's flank with his boot, moving into a smooth, rocking canter as he focused on the distant stone wall. His muscular body moved with the gelding, his thighs gripping the saddle, and his hands resting lightly on the reins. Still in training, Verity had been worth every pound. He had heart and courage and would gallop over a cliff if asked.

Marked as a rogue and a bone-setter at Tattersall's auction, the horse had apparently refused to bend under training or listen to the whip. But the gelding's eyes had held intelligence when Gideon stroked his wavy dark forelock and blew gently on his nose. The "beast" turned out to have more common sense than most of those roughriders, who thought to break an animal's spirit with fear and domination. The three-year-old wanted to please but had rebelled against unwarranted pain. The fading scars that marked the ebony hide from sharp spurs and countless lashes proved it had not been the proper incentive. Verity enjoyed a challenge and learned quickly when asked with kindness. Animals weren't much different from people really, except perhaps more trustworthy.

The pair approached the hedgerow. Gideon leaned forward and grabbed a fistful of mane with his spur hand. A subtle cue and the horse sailed over the shrub, landing gracefully on the other side. The wind pulled at the opening in his shirt, and it billowed around him with a flapping noise. He gave Verity a pat on the neck and eased him into a trot. "Good boy!"

The cool morning breeze lifted the hair off Gideon's neck and cooled the sweat running down his back. The sweet smell of fresh-cut hay filled the air and he breathed deeply. His eyes swept over the green pastures and dotted hills that had claimed his imagination as a child. Playing with the village children and fighting dragons on ancient ponies, looking for buried treasure, or going to war against the Danes or the French—depending on the most recent history lesson. Where had that adventurous youth gone?

Verity's ears pricked forward. Gideon chuckled at the scruffy little brown mutt bounding up the hill. "Good morn to you, Little Bit."

The dog barked in reply, his tail wagging so rapidly that it seemed a blur. "A race, you say?" Little

Bit barked his agreement. "I'll tell you what. I'll keep him in a trot to make it fair."

The threesome ambled west, their backs to the sun. They crested a hill and the sight of his childhood home in the distance, standing sentry over the countryside, filled Gideon with pride. The numerous windows of the imposing three-story medieval manor glinted and flashed like jewels in a crown of gray sandstone. On each corner, gable, and the entrance sat miniature turrets like arrows pointing to the heavens. Surrounded by the original moat, it reminded visitors of long-gone knights, fair maidens, and chivalry. A wide, arched bridge spanned the ditch, bricks matching the color of the mansion and providing ample entrance to the estate grounds. Rolling hills and grazing pastures surrounded the mansion on three sides with acres of forest along the back. From atop this hill, it was an impressive sight, and Gideon always enjoyed watching people's reaction the first time they saw it.

Little Bit barked, tail wagging and feet pawing at his stirrup. "My father passed on quite a legacy, didn't he? Now it's up to me to maintain and improve it."

He leaned down to give the dog a final scratch then headed down the hill at an easy canter, mentally ticking off the correspondence he would respond to after breakfast. The estate's steward also wanted to update him on some newly acquired livestock. There was the appointment with the solicitor next week in London concerning the textile mill in Glasgow. The business had been his father's personal project so Gideon was eager to learn more about the details of that particular investment. It was the only corner of the Stanfeld holdings the late earl had seen to himself.

London. The visit would be a two-edged sword. On one hand, he looked forward to a few nights of gaming and camaraderie with good friends. Perhaps a stop at Tattersall's to see what was on the auction block. On the other hand, those voracious, title-seeking mothers with their simpering single daughters... At least the families were sparser this time of year. At twenty-five, he still enjoyed his bachelor status and tried to avoid the town in the spring and early summer as carefully as horse piles on a busy street.

Just before crossing the bridge, he dismounted. Little Bit rushed ahead, barking a warning that his master was home. Gideon paused beneath one of the yew trees flanking the bridge, tucked his shirt into his breeches, and rolled down his sleeves. The reddish brown bark shown with purple in the morning light, and the low hanging branches swayed softly in the breeze. He walked across the bridge, buttoning his cuffs, his boot heels clicking against the bricks. The water below sparkled as lilies floated lazily along, an occasional fish making a splash. A stable hand waited on the steps, holding a crust of bread out to the dog.

"Give him a long rubdown. He worked hard this morning." Gideon gave the horse another pat on its muscular neck and handed over the reins.

"Yes, my lord." The man led the animal away, the tatty pup at his heels.

Sanders, the butler, greeted him at the door. "Good day, my lord. Lady Stanfeld is waiting for you." His gray eyes, matching his thinning hair, danced with humor as he collected his lord's waistcoat, crop, and gloves. "She appears to be making a list."

Gideon groaned. "Of females?"

"Yes, my lord, I'm afraid so."

"Thank you, Sanders." Gideon ignored the family portraits and the suit of armor stoically standing guard as he strode through the entryway. Intent on changing before greeting his mother, he bounded up the circular staircase two steps at a time.

Gideon entered his chambers, finished a quick half-bath, and wiped dry with a clean linen towel. He dressed in fresh buckskin breeches, a white cambric shirt, a brandy-colored waistcoat, and finished tying his cravat as he hurried down the stairs.

"Good morning, dear Mama," he murmured as he bent low to kiss her cheek. "You look fetching in that deep shade of lavender. I'm happy to see you finally out of those blacks. It doesn't suit you."

"I've followed the English tradition of mourning in honor of your father. But I'm happy to have some color back. It brightens the skin." Her words still held the barest hint of a Scottish accent. Maeve smoothed her crepe skirt and smiled. "I've been waiting for you."

"So I've been told. Perhaps some coffee before you bombard me with your list?" Gideon smirked at her surprised look until those dark blue eyes flashed with determination. He held up a hand. "I'll listen with interest as soon as I've finished a cup and had something to eat."

Maeve watched in bemused silence as a servant poured the steaming black liquid into a china cup. Gideon lathered soft butter onto a thick slice of fresh bread and scooped some cherry preserves on top. With a groan of delight, he chewed with his eyes closed and finished with a smack of his lips. "This season's cherries were superb."

Maeve opened her mouth then closed it as he reached for his coffee. She made a face.

"And is that displeasure aimed at me, Mama?"

She shook her head. "I don't know how you can prefer that horrible drink to tea. And without even a drop of milk or lump of sugar."

He grinned, spearing a piece of cold beef with his fork. "I have my father's dour demeanor and prefer the bitter to the sweet. Now, who is on your marriage agenda?"

She frowned. "It is not an agenda or about marriage. I've decided to have a small dinner party, and I've listed a few names that might be of interest."

The last thing Gideon wanted was to be surrounded by tiresome young ladies looking for a husband. But seeing the light back in his mother's eyes, he kept his thoughts to himself. It had been over a year since she had accepted an invitation or entertained. He was willing to be the sacrificial lamb to see her reenter society.

"I am happy to play host for whatever event you would like to arrange. Now about that list..."

His mind wandered as she told him of the families that would receive an invitation. His father had endured these social affairs as a matter of course. Always the proper gentleman, always the mannered aristocrat, always the impassive Englishman. Life was a set of rules and one followed those tenets to the letter in private, in social circles, and in business. The world, according to the late earl, was black and white.

The exception had been his wife, the vibrant and outspoken Maeve of the prominent Clan MacNaughton. The earl had disliked the superstitious and rebellious Highlanders but had fallen in love with one of the chieftain's daughters. She had seemed to be the only weakness in his inflexible world, the only person or thing he allowed to let him stray from society's rigid rules. Gideon had seen her pull caps with him and hold her own, occasionally even winning an argument. Those instances had ended with a wicked glint in his father's eyes and a smug smile on his mother's lips. Then the two of them would hide away in their bedchamber the rest of the day.

"I received a letter from Marietta last week. She'd like to visit before winter. So I will plan it as a welcome dinner in September. She's finally with child, you know. It may be quite some time before she can travel again."

The last words sounded wistful and brought Gideon back to the conversation. Marietta, the eldest sister, was less than two years behind him. Then came Charlotte, four years his junior, and Helen the youngest at eighteen. All had married well, in their father's opinion, with the exception of Helen. She had wed a wealthy base-born Irishman. "It will be good to see Etta again. I'm surprised Lord Burnham is allowing her out of his sight. After three years, I swear the man is still smelling of April and May."

"There is nothing wrong with being in love. And he'll most certainly keep a close eye on that girl." Maeve laughed. "She's still a bit impetuous, but motherhood will slow her down."

"I hope something does." He rose from the table and kissed Maeve again on the cheek. "I will leave you to your preparations, then. I'll be with the steward for the rest of the day. "

The accounts for the quarter completed, Gideon and Jethro Birks admired the sheep littering the grassy hillside. They were fine stock and his steward had finagled an excellent price the previous year. "Outstanding job. I'm impressed with the results of the spring shearing. Damn good wool and damn good profits."

"It took some talking, my lord, but I finally convinced your father to let me bring in these sheep from Gower. Much better quality than the Vale long wool and brings twice the price." The summer sun had bleached Jethro's hair almost white, making his brown eyes and tanned skin appear even darker. He pointed in the direction of a southern pasture. "I'd like to try grazing the cattle same as the sheep. Get the animals out of the yards, and we'll see better milk and beef."

"With your past record, I'm inclined to trust your judgment on this. By god, you even managed a second hay cutting this summer. There'll be plenty of feed for the winter."

"Can't take all the credit for that, my lord. The weather helped a bit."

Gideon looked over the acreage with a contented smile, his father's words coming to mind. *Surround yourself with competent men, treat them well, and your land and finances will prosper.*

This was proof of that philosophy. He'd known Jethro since they were boys, hunting squirrel with slingshots and swimming in the horse pond. He was the third generation of Birks to manage the Stanfeld estates, and Gideon was thankful to have such a downy steward.

"I'll be in London for a few days, checking in with the solicitor. Fair warning"—he cleared his throat—"Lady Stanfeld has come out of mourning and is planning a country party for September. What she has described as a small dinner gathering will no doubt turn into a week of company."

"Yes, my lord. Consider me prepared for the upcoming requests."

"Give my regards to your charming wife." Gideon turned his gelding back toward the manor. It had been a productive day, and he was ready for a glass of sherry and a good meal.

The Countess of Stanfeld settled into her favorite chair near the library hearth. She held a small book of poems and read a few pages until her eyes grew weary. Her thoughts strayed to her late husband Charles and the heart condition that had sapped his strength his last years. It had made him weak of body but not weak of mind. He had remained lucid and pragmatic until the end, knowing death was upon him and looking the reaper in the eye. Maeve had always admired his supreme will and saw that same strength in her children.

But he had also been a narrow-minded man in a sense, whose rational views did not allow him to see anything except what lay in front of him. If it was not factual or quantifiable, it was not real. He had laughed at her first vision of a sinking ship he planned to invest in, indulging her recount as if it were an amusing story. Until it came true. It had shaken the very foundation of everything he considered Truth. Rather than look too deeply into the situation, he shunned the unexplainable. Ran from it as if it were the devil himself after his soul.

His reaction had been swift and irrevocable. Her female mind was too easily swayed by homeland folklore. Maeve would not return to the Highlands while there was breath left in him. She would remain in England, become a proper countess, and forget the mystical nonsense of her childhood. By that time, she loved him so deeply that the fear in his eyes had frightened her also. He didn't understand, didn't have the capability to conceive of something so intangible, other than God. And he struggled with that omniscient presence. So she never told him of another vision, and instead did what she could to avoid tragedy whenever possible. She willingly gave up her childhood home for him but refused to give up her family.

The earl had compromised with his wife and in-laws by going to the Scottish Lowlands and meeting in Glasgow twice a year. The couple had first been introduced in that city, when Charles and her father, Calum MacNaughton, had met to discuss the purchase of a textile mill. Her father still insisted the papers had only been signed after Maeve had agreed to his courtship. The trips satisfied the desire for her children to know the MacNaughton clan. Gideon had always been especially close to his grandfather, growing more like his image every year with Calum's muscular build, black hair, and piercing blue eyes.

She smiled, closed her eyes, and gave in to a pleasant afternoon nap.

He pushed against the throng of men, women, and children to hear the gentleman on the stage. The stink of unwashed bodies and a hum of excitement filled the air. He pulled off his waistcoat as the sweat pooled beneath his collar. The speaker's words of reform and the right to vote echoed in his head and filled him with purpose.

A woman holding a small child sidled up next to him, a smile on her lips. The pair made him think of his own wife and the family they would have. The wee girl had the same dimples as her mother. The babe waved a hand at him, and he caught her chubby fingers in his. Grasping her mother's braid in her other hand, the babe sucked heartily then began to cry as the noise increased. She squealed as the crowd jostled the pair and reached toward him. The pressure of bodies behind them intensified, and the hair on the back of his neck rose. Something wasna right.

Screams pierced the air, and he turned to see the cause of such panic. Mounted Hussars stormed the assembly, the rhythmic whisk of blades slicing the air. A glistening black beast, eyes rolling, lunged forward then reared. Flying hooves pawed at the scrambling bodies and struck the infant in the head. The mother screamed, her arms reaching for the falling child.

He pushed the frantic woman away from the soldier's sword then threw himself on the tiny, lifeless form. "Ye bloody bastards," he cried as the horse reared once again.

This time its full weight landed on his back. The crack of bone echoed in his ears. Excruciating pain exploded along the length of his body. From the ground, he saw a jumble of feet and hooves, all moving in different directions. A man's face— contorted in pain—trampled by the frantic feet escaping the massacre. He tried to hunch over the child still beneath him, protect it from the stampede, but his body had been flattened. An image flashed of the local butcher pounding a tough piece of meat.

A blow to his head...a piercing throb... Then the world spun in slow motion. The shrieks of victims *and harsh shouts of the soldiers came from far away now. Another image. His sweet wife's face.*

"I'm so verra sorry, Lissie..." he whispered.

———

Gideon entered the library, still warm from the afternoon sun. Mama sat before the fireplace, the large wingback almost swallowing up her small frame. She had aged in the last year. A few streaks of gray now blended with the rich auburn hair. Her eyes were closed, but her lids fluttered as if dreaming. The sapphire ring, a wedding gift from her husband that matched her eyes, glinted and winked as her slender fingers gripped and released the armchair. Her head rocked back and forth as Gideon squatted down next to her. His fingers covered hers, and he squeezed to wake her from such troubled sleep. The touch sent a jolt through her body. Her eyes snapped open.

"No!" she gasped, her gaze fixed on the darkened hearth.

"Mama, you were dreaming." His thumb stroked the top of her hand, his voice soft and soothing. "Look at me, Mama, and you will see."

Maeve slowly turned her head, tears now spilling down her cheeks. "Oh Gideon, it was ghastly."

"What did you dream?"

"It was not a dream." Her voice faltered. "Your cousin, Ian, is dead."

"What? Did you receive a letter from Scotland?" Gideon had not seen any correspondence from his mother's family over the last week, and nothing had arrived today.

"I do not need a letter. I saw it. There's been a terrible slaughter in Manchester, and Ian was trampled..." She lifted her chin and wiped at her wet cheeks with determination. "You must take me home to my clan."

"To the Highlands? You haven't been there since your wedding." He sighed and rubbed the back of his neck. "I can't just run off to Scotland with my aging mother because of a dream."

"Aging?" Her eyes narrowed, anger shining from beneath her lashes. "I have more stamina than most of those mutton-headed females of the *ton*."

He had to agree with her but bit back a smile. "This is folly. A trick of the mind from lack of sleep." He pressed his lips to her fingers. "Let's have a glass of sherry, and you'll feel better after we eat."

"Don't patronize me. Your father didn't believe in..." She took his face in both her hands, strength growing in her touch and her gaze steady and direct. "It doesn't matter. Listen to me. It was not a dream but a message of sorts that we are needed at home."

"This is our home." Gideon stood and leaned an arm against the fireplace mantel, worried the past year had also taken a toll on her mind. An uprising in Manchester? There had been rumblings throughout parts of the country but nothing significant.

"This is *your* home. *Mine* has always been in Scotland, regardless of how long I've been away." Her eyes pleaded with him.

"What about Marietta's visit in September?" That would end this foolishness, he was sure.

"It will have to wait until October. You must promise we will leave as soon as you return from London. Or I will go alone."

He looked up to the ceiling, hoping for some divine intervention. None came. "I give you my word."

About the Author

Bestselling and award-winning author Aubrey Wynne resides in the Midwest with her husband, dogs, horses, mule and barn cats. She is an elementary teacher by trade, champion of children and animals by conscience, and author by night. Obsessions include history, travel, trail riding and all things Christmas.

Her short stories, **_Merry Christmas, Henry and Pete's Mighty Purty Privies_** have won Readers Choice Awards. **_Dante's Gift_** and **_Paper Love_** received the 2016 Golden Quill, Aspen Gold, Heart of Excellence and the Gayle Wilson Award of Excellence.

In addition to her Chicago Christmas novellas, Aubrey will release two more Regency romances in 2018. The Wicked Earls' Club will release again in 2019. Wynne's medieval fantasy series launched in 2017 with **_Rolf's Quest_**, winner of the NTRWA Great Expectations.

More Historical Romance by Aubrey Wynne

Regency Romance

Earl of Sunderland (Once Upon a Widow #1) (Wicked Earls' Club)

http://aubreywynne.com/book/earl-of-sunderland/

"Well-written historical romance with a bit of everything – a tragedy, a conflicted hero, a strong and fragile heroine, interesting characters, and a happily ever after." *–Verified review*

"Best Regency Romance I've read in a long time and highly recommend!" *–N.N. Light Book Heaven Reviews*

"I adored this story. I look forward to reading more in this series." *–Reads2Love Review*

"A wonderful romance!" –5 Kindles Review

Grace Beaumont has seen what love can do to a woman. Her mother sacrificed her life to produce the coveted son and heir. A devastated father and newborn brother force her to take on the role of Lady Boldon at the age of fifteen. But Grace finds solace in the freedom and power of her new status.

Christopher Roker made a name for himself in the military. The rigor and pragmatism of the army suits him. When a tragic accident heaves Kit into a role he never wanted or expected, his world collides with another type of duty. Returning to England and his newfound responsibilities, the Wicked Earls' Club becomes a refuge from the glitter and malice of London society but cannot ease his emptiness.

Needing an escape from his late brother's memory and reputation, Kit visits the family estate for the summer. Lady Grace, a beauty visiting from a neighboring estate, becomes a welcome distraction. When the chance to return to the military becomes a valid possibility, the earl finds himself wavering between his old life and the lure of an exceptional—and unwilling—woman.

A Wicked Earl's Widow (Once Upon a Widow #2)

http://aubreywynne.com/book/a-wicked-earls-widow/

When Eliza's abusive father forced her into marriage, she had no idea her life would change for the better. Married less than a year, her unwilling rake of a husband had been surprisingly kind to her—until his sudden death. The widowed Countess of Sunderland is more than happy to remain with her in-laws and raise their daughter. Unfortunately, her own family is on the brink of financial ruin and has other plans.

Nathaniel, Viscount of Pendleton, gained his title at the age of 12. His kindly but astute estate manager became father and mentor, instilling in the boy an astute sense of responsibility and compassion for his tenants. Fifteen years later, his family urges him to visit London and seek a wife. The ideal doesn't appeal to him, but his sense of duty tells him it is the next logical step.

When Lord Pendleton stumbles upon Eliza on the road, defending an elderly woman against ruffians, he's shocked and intrigued. After rescuing the exquisite damsel in distress, he finds himself smitten. But Nate soon realizes he must discover the dark secrets of her past to truly save the woman he loves.

Rhapsody and Rebellion (Once Upon a Widow #3) (Enduring Legacy #7)

http://aubreywynne.com/book/rhapsody-and-rebellion/

An enduring legacy... A rebellion... A destined love...

Raised in his father's image—practical and disciplined—there are no gray lines interrupting the Earl of Stanfeld's black and white world. Until his mother has a dream and begs to return to her Highland home.

Alisabeth was betrothed from the cradle. At seventeen, she marries her best friend and finds happiness if not passion. In less than a year, she's a widow. Vowing to honor her husband's memory, she joins his activist group of Glasgow weavers and is soon embroiled in the Radical War of 1820.

Crossing the border into Scotland, Gideon finds his predictable world turned upside down. Folklore, legend, and political unrest intertwine with an unexpected attraction to a feisty Highland beauty. But Lissie doesn't trust the Englishman or the rising desire between them. When the earl learns of an English plot to stir the Scots into rebellion, he must choose his country or save the clan and the woman that stirs his soul.

Medieval Romance

Rolf's Quest (A Medieval Encounter #1)

http://aubreywynne.com/aubreys-
books/aubreys-historical-romance/

****Great Expectations winner, Fire & Ice
finalist, Maggie finalist****

"Author Aubrey Wynne brings a swashbuckling
epic story of family, love and betrayal to life in "Rolf's
Quest". The structure of the story is done well -- it is
long on action and moves at breakneck speed. The
plot is perfectly paced, with characters that will pull
the reader right into the action. They are likable and
readers will root for Rolf and Melissa throughout
their struggles. The strength of their bond will keep
readers glued to their seat right until the very last
page. Hold onto your helmet, readers, and grab a
shield -- Rolf is just around the corner." –*InD'tale
magazine*

"This was a surprisingly smooth read that I flew
through in practically one sitting. I loved how easily
I was immersed in this medieval world filled with
royalty, knights, wizards, and villains. The magical
element was interesting and I liked the way Merlin's
story was woven into this book. The plot sucked me
in and I thoroughly enjoyed following Rolf's journey.

In closing... A story with pretty much everything
a fantasy romance fan can want. 4.5 stars" –
Romance Reviews

A wizard, a curse, a fated love...

When Rolf finally discovers the woman who can end the curse that has plagued his family for centuries, she is already betrothed. Time is running out for the royal wizard of King Henry II. If he cannot find true love without the use of sorcery, the magic will die for future generations.

Melissa is intrigued by the mystical, handsome man who haunts her by night and tempts her by day. His bizarre tale of Merlin, enchantments, and finding genuine love has her questioning his sanity and her heart.

From the moment Melissa stepped from his dreams and into his arms, Rolf knew she was his destiny. Now, he will battle against time, a powerful duke, and call on the gods to save her.

Saving Grace (A Small Town Romance)
http://aubreywynne.com/book/saving-grace/

Contemporary and Colonial America

Holt and Maggie award finalist

This unique piece has the reader traveling between the early 1700s and the early 2000s with ease and amazement. The audience truly feels sorrow for Grace and Chloe and is able to connect with each woman for the hardships they are overcoming... The attention to historical facts and details leave one breathless, especially upon learning the people from the past did exist and the memorial erected still stands. *–InD'tale Magazine*

"I am becoming a pretty decent fan of the author I would say at this point. She managed in such a short amount of pages to thrill me with some lore, romance, and suspense." –*Amazon review*

A tortured soul meets a shattered heart...

Chloe Hicks' life consisted of an egocentric ex-husband, a pile of bills, and an equine business in foreclosure until a fire destroys the stable and her beloved ranch horse. What little hope she has left is smashed after the marshal suspects arson. She escapes the accusing eyes of her hometown, but not the memories and melancholy.

Jackson Hahn, Virginia Beach's local historian, has his eyes on the mysterious new woman in town. When she enters his office, he is struck by her haunting beauty and the raw pain in her eyes. Her descriptions of the odd events happening in her bungalow pique his curiosity.

The sexy historian distracts Chloe with the legend of a woman wrongly accused of witchcraft. She is drawn to the story and the similarities of events that plagued their lives. Perhaps the past can help heal the present. But danger lurks in the shadows...

A Chicago Christmas
(Sweet Holiday Novella Series)

http://aubreywynne.com/book/dantes-gift-a-chicago-christmas-1/

Dante's Gift (Chicago Christmas #1)
Contemporary and WWII

Winner of the Golden Quill, Aspen Gold and Heart of Excellence RWA awards, Rone Award finalist in Audio

"Wynne has crafted a a beautiful short story guaranteed to warm your heart and make you sigh." –Kishan Paul, *Second Wife Series*

"...a wonderfully poignant holiday romantic tale that intertwines two love stories..." –Jersey Girls Book Reviews

"A lovely sweet romance!" –Book Addicts

Kathleen James has put her practical side away for once and looks forward to the perfect romantic evening: an intimate dinner with the man of her dreams—and an engagement ring. She is not prepared to hear that he wants to bring his grandmother back from Italy to live with him.

Dominic Lawrence has planned this marriage proposal for six months. Nothing can go wrong—until his Nonna calls. Now he must interrupt the tenderest night of Katie's life with the news that another woman will be under their roof.

When Antonia's sister dies, she finds herself longing to be back in the states. An Italian wartime bride from the '40s, she knows how precious love can be. Can her own story of an American soldier and a very special collie once again bring two hearts together at Christmas?

For the Love of Laura Beth (Chicago Christmas #4)

http://aubreywynne.com/book/laura-beth/

2019 Rone Finalist, InD'Tale Magazine
Maggie finalist, Book Buyers Best

"Beautifully written and tells a story that will allow readers to experience the turmoil that war can bring to the lives of those who must endure its heartbreak." –Amazon Review

"This isn't your typical boy-meets-girl-they-get-married-and-live-happily-ever-after-the-end story. This is sweet romance in the midst of real life hardships and pain, and a love that will press through and triumph." –Amazon Review

The Korean War destroyed their plans, but the battle at home may shatter their hearts...

Laura Beth Walters fell in love with Joe McCall when she was six years old. Now she is counting the days until Joey graduates from college so they can marry and begin their life together. But the Korean War rips their neatly laid plans to shreds. Instead of a college fraternity, Joey joins a platoon. Laura Beth trades a traditional wedding for a quick trip to the courthouse.

They endure the hardships of separation, but the true battle is faced when Joey returns from the war. Their devotion is soon tested beyond endurance. Joe and Laura Beth must find a way to accept the trials thrown in their path and remain steadfast, or lose their faith and each other.